Flee, Fly, Flown

A NOVEL

Flee, Fly, Flown

JANET HEPBURN

Second Story Press

Library and Archives Canada Cataloguing in Publication

Hepburn, Janet
Flee, fly, flown / Janet Hepburn.

Issued also in an electronic format.
ISBN 978-1-927583-03-6

I. Title.

PS8615.E67F54 2013   C813'.6   C2012-908173-6

Edited by Kathryn Cole
Cover: Illustration © Greg Stevenson/www.i2iart.com
Design by Melissa Kaita

Printed and bound in Canada

Second Story Press gratefully acknowledges the support of the Ontario Arts Council and the Canada Council for the Arts for our publishing program. We acknowledge the financial support of the Government of Canada through the Canada Book Fund.

 ONTARIO ARTS COUNCIL
CONSEIL DES ARTS DE L'ONTARIO

 Canada Council   Conseil des Arts
for the Arts   du Canada

 MIX
Paper from
responsible sources
FSC
www.fsc.org   FSC® C004071

Published by
SECOND STORY PRESS
20 Maud Street, Suite 401
Toronto, ON M5V 2M5
www.secondstorypress.ca

For my mother
Anna Mary Greenslade, 1921–2011,
paragon of extraordinary strength and courage
through a decade spent living with Alzheimer's

Part I

Flee

The Nursing Home

1

I SLIDE MY PLATE to the center of the table, put down my fork, and lean toward Audrey. "I can't eat one more bite of this tasteless mush. I need giant chunks of toffee."

Audrey continues to eat as if I'm not here.

"Audrey?" I tap her arm to get her attention.

She raises only her eyes in my direction. "What did you say?"

"Good grief," I mumble under my breath, "where is that damn waiter, anyway?" Then loudly to Audrey, "I said I'm gonna move out, pull up stakes, hit the road if I don't get something decent to eat soon."

She pushes the food around on her plate; selects the perfect combination of colors on her fork—white, orange, green—all tinged gray from too much time in the warming trays. "You always say that, but you're still here," she says. "Where would you go?"

I gaze around the room at all the faces and surroundings, familiar now but not always. "I want to go home."

The dining room is filled with gray-haired women and a spattering of balding men. The space between tables is cluttered with wheelchairs and walkers. Pastel uniforms with white sneakers perch on stools, spooning food into random open mouths like mother birds feeding their young. They write on clipboards, recording how much we eat, how much we leave behind. At least that's what they say. Maybe they're writing stories or letters to their sisters, or maybe they're drawing funny pictures of us to laugh at with their friends.

A mint-green uniform stops at our table and takes away my untouched dinner. She sets a bowl of Jell-O in front of me. "There you go," she says.

There I go, indeed. These rubbery cubes are about the last thing I want, but I've learned the right response; "Thank you, Dear."

A shiver trickles down my back. I wrap my sweater tighter around my shoulders and watch as Audrey tries to eat her pudding with a fork.

"Are you cold?" the uniform asks. "It's August and it's hot out there. You're lucky to be in here with the air conditioning."

She makes a fanning gesture with her hand and walks away.

I stare at the neon-orange Jell-O and sip my tea. "Audrey!" I holler to make myself heard. "It's August. Do you know what that means?"

Audrey looks at me with a puzzled expression. "I know what August is. What are you getting at?"

"We need to get out of here—go on a vacation.

4

It's August so we should go soon, before it turns cool. Would you go with me?"

Audrey brightens. "Yes."

The woman across the table drops her plate and it clatters across the floor. Audrey tries to push it back to her using the tip of her cane.

My mind is humming. "We should drive." I keep talking, a plan splatting from my lips, surprising me as much as it does Audrey. "Do you have a car?"

"Do I hafflegar?" Audrey asks.

"Good Lord! You need new batteries in your hearing aid. A *car*. Do you have a car?"

"No, I don't think so." She pauses, looking around the room. "No. I sold my car to the boy who lives next door. Nice young man. He was just learning to drive."

"Carol and Tom sold my car too, along with my house and everything else I owned." I can feel my voice rising and my shoulders tightening. "I'm sure they stole all my money too. That's why they don't visit. They keep telling me they're *looking after* my money for me. Bullshit!" I take a deep breath like the uniforms always tell me to. "*Think about something else*," they say. "*Think about nice things.*"

"Albert would never have let this happen. He would have sat those kids down and given them a stern talking-to. They listened to him too, much more than to me."

Audrey heaves herself up with the help of her cane. She's shorter and rounder than I am, and wobbly on her right leg, but she gets around pretty well with her walking stick. And she is sweet—like Fraise, my aunt. I couldn't have made it growing up without Fraise. I think about her

5

all the time and how she took care of me when my mother couldn't be bothered.

Audrey hobbles over to me and rubs my back. "It's okay, Hon. We don't need them. We'll figure out a way."

I wipe my eyes with my sleeve and pull a pen from my sweater pocket. On a napkin, I scribble the word *vacation*. Twice. I tear the napkin in two and give one piece to Audrey. I fold the other and place it carefully in my pocket beside the pen. "So we don't forget," I say. "This is important."

It's morning and on my way to the dining room for breakfast, I spot Audrey sitting on her bed, rifling through a leather purse the size of a full-grown cat. She looks up and waves.

"Come in here for a minute. Sit down." She continues to pull things out of the various pockets and compartments in the purse and lay them on the bed beside the napkin with the one-word reminder, *vacation*.

"Aaahaa!"

She pulls a set of keys from one of the zippered pockets and jangles them in my direction. "I think that one of these is the extra key to my car. I found this purse stuck in the back of my closet and look what was hiding inside!" She holds the keys in one hand and reaches over to pick up the napkin with the other.

"What luck," I say, cupping one hand around the keys and shaking her hand with the other.

Audrey gathers the items from the bed to put them back in the leather cat. Her face lights up again. "And look what else I found." She pulls a wad of bills from a clear plastic change purse tucked in the bottom of the bag. "Ta-da!"

"You are really something!" I tell her. "Now we have a car and money. I'm sure I'll remember how to drive once I'm behind the wheel."

A pair of men's shoes and pant legs appear around the edge of the doorway followed in short bursts by a wheelchair carrying a plump, gray-haired man with a pasty complexion. The man looks at me for some time before he speaks.

"I'm Harry," he says in a low, scratchy voice.

"Hello, Harry. We know who you are."

He focuses more closely on our faces. "What are you doing?"

"Talking about women's problems—you know—arm flab, whiskers, vaginal dryness. Do you mind? It's kind of personal," I say, looking him straight in the eye.

Harry spins around with new agility and wheels away quicker than a young pup caught piddling on the rug.

Audrey stifles a laugh. "Pervert! That was fast thinking!"

I laugh. "I don't know where the dryness came from. I can't remember the last time I worried about that."

Breakfast is over. Porridge, toast, scrambled eggs. Who can eat that much of the same thing, day after day? Audrey taps her cane on the floor and stands up. "Let's go play some bingo."

At the elevators, we push the button and wait.

"Where are you going Lillian? Audrey?" someone asks from the nearby desk.

"Downstairs to bingo."

As the elevator door opens, an alarm starts to chime. Inside, we push buttons but the door stays open. The chime persists.

A uniform rises from her chair behind the desk and joins

us. "No one leaves the floor without a staff member." She enters a code on the keypad. "We don't want anyone wandering off, do we?"

The door closes and we drop. My stomach does a loop-de-loop.

"Why does the elevator work for you but not for us?" I ask.

Her glance darts toward my wrist, then back up to meet my eye. "It's magic. The elevator just knows when there's someone in it that isn't supposed to leave the floor."

"We're old and sometimes forgetful. That doesn't mean we've totally lost our grip on reality," I say. "No need to be conde…hensive."

The elevator opens onto a large room filled with chairs and tables and more gray hair. The uniform holds the door and waves until she gets the attention of the bingo-caller. Everyone stops and stares, some at us and some just gazing into space, as we find seats and wait for our bingo cards and dabbers. I touch my wrist and feel the familiar bracelet. It says *SafeChip* on the band. Around the room, I'm surprised to see that each person wears the same thing. The blue squares and white bands are so conspicuous that I wonder why I haven't noticed them before.

A tall man wearing a ridiculous looking blue pinny that says "Volunteers are the heart of good healthcare" (the word *heart* replaced with a huge red valentine shape), leans over and tapes a bingo card to the table.

"Tell me something," I say quietly. I point to the wristband. "Does this thing make the alarm go off in the elevator?"

He looks surprised at the question. "You're very bright." He hands me a dabber and moves off toward Audrey.

I'm sitting in a chair near the elevators, watching visitors come and go. Uniforms travel up and down from floor to floor and the alarms don't sound. Finally, when no one is around, I push the button and stand close to the door as it opens. There it is—*bing, bing, bing.* I hurry away and wander the halls until I find Audrey, standing beside the aquarium, watching the fish.

I hold out my arm so Audrey can see. "We need to chuck these bracelets."

She looks confused. "I'm not sure." She touches the one on her own arm. "I've got one too. Is it some sort of watch?"

"We need to get rid of them," I tell her, my voice growing louder. "They set off the alarm in the elevator. We'll never be able to sneak out as long as we're wearing these." Sometimes Audrey just doesn't get it.

"What do you mean, sneak out?"

I reach into my sweater pocket, take out the napkin, and hold it up for Audrey to read.

"Oh! Of course." She takes hold of her wristband and pulls. She scrunches her hand up as narrow as she can and tries to work the bracelet off. It doesn't budge. "We need scissors."

I nod. "Exactly." I look around the room. "They never let us have anything shiny. We'll have to steal them."

Audrey looks puzzled. "Shiny?"

"You know—to cut with—shiny." A spasm of pain in my back leaves me suddenly weak. "I need to sit down."

We join some other women in the comfortable chairs clustered in front of the television. Some are dozing, others stare at the dark screen. Soon Audrey and I are doing the same.

"Do you want the TV on?" a blue-pinnyed woman asks as she walks through the room.

No one responds.

The room suddenly fills with color and sound. The blue pinny puts down the switcher-thing and continues on her way.

Noise and nonsense is all I hear. The characters on the screen look like clowns, their movements exaggerated. They talk too fast. It hurts my eyes and ears.

I walk a lot. I'm free when I'm walking around and around the loop of hallway that joins all of our rooms. I don't need to ask permission or ask for help. I'm on my own. On the second time around the loop, I spot my quilt in one of the rooms. It's purple and green and no one else has one like it, thank God. People always get mad when I lie on their beds by mistake. I go in and stretch out on my quilt, almost paralyzed by the pain stabbing through my back. I roll onto my side, and after a moment, I'm surprised to find a warm, wet spot on my pillow just beneath my cheek. Tears. It seems I'm leaking from everywhere these days.

I slept poorly last night, but this morning I'm wide awake, dying for a cup of hot coffee, wishing I could drink it from a pottery mug instead of the thermal plastic cup with the sippy lid. I look around for my table—the one assigned to me. A woman waves—Eleanor, I think. She doesn't speak English. For all I know, she could be swearing at me. She pats the seat beside her, inviting me to sit, then lets loose in long, expressive streams of words, waving her hands and smoothing her skirt over the dark woolen stockings she wears, even through the summer. Another woman sits on the other side, a little thing with frizzy, bleached hair and crooked teeth. And Audrey is here.

I'm drawn to Audrey more than the others at Tranquil Meadows Nursing Home. We came to live here around the same time, though heaven knows when that was. Days and months are no longer distinguishable, one from the other, in this place. The chalkboard behind the workers' station declares it is Saturday, August 5.

During breakfast, the woman in charge of keeping us busy with silly games and repetitive singsongs—I've forgotten her name—zigzags between the tables, inviting each person to come to the recreation room to make "late summer bouquets from fabric and pipe cleaners and seed pods."

I finger the crumpled bit of napkin in my pocket. "Audrey," I say.

Audrey looks up and smiles. "New batteries," she says, pointing at her hearing aid.

"Great! There's a craft class this morning."

Audrey looks back at her bowl and scoops a spoonful of oatmeal into her mouth. She swallows and says, "I don't feel like it today."

I reach over and point at the wristband on her arm. "It's a craft class. There'll be scissors."

"Scissors?" She stares blankly at her wristband.

"To cut these off," I remind her. "To cut our way to freedom. You need to focus. Try to remember the plan at all times."

The activities lady is still talking. "You can go back to your rooms and get ready. We'll come and pick you up in half an hour to take you downstairs," she announces to anyone who will listen.

Audrey rises and nods at me. "See you down there then?"

"Definitely. I wouldn't miss the making of late summer

bouffants for anything." I march down the hall in search of my room.

I open all the drawers in my cupboard and move things around. My toothbrush is gone. I finally find it stored along with some toothpaste in a small drawer in the bathroom. How did it get there? This must be a new drawer. I find my comb in the same place, soak it under running water, and rake it through my hair. A quick look in the mirror, then I turn and open the door.

A middle-aged woman stands in my room, dark brown hair pulled back in a clip and narrow glasses in shades of brown and yellow perched on her nose. "Mother—there you are," she says. The woman strides over, bends down, and wraps her arms around me.

I feel my body tense. "Carol? What are you doing here?"

2

CAROL'S SMILE FADES. Her arms fall to her sides. "Nice greeting! Glad to see you too, Mom."

I take her hand in both of mine. "I'm sorry, Dear. You surprised me, that's all. I didn't know you were coming."

"Don't you remember? Last time I visited, we set up this date to go shopping for shoes and some new clothes for you."

"We did?" I glance at the clock. I can hear the staff circulating to escort people to the craft room. "Oh dear, I'm afraid I can't go this morning. Could you come back this afternoon?"

"No, Mom, I can't. I need to head back to Toronto by mid-afternoon. I thought we could shop this morning, have a bite to eat, then I'd bring you back here and go. What's so important that you have to do this morning?"

I try to come up with a reason that will sound important, but the words just won't come and I settle on a partial truth.

"We're making late summer bouquets."

Carol looks relieved. "Oh, good Lord. Surely you can miss that?"

"No. No, I can't. We have to go. It's mandible." I sit on the bed and hope someone will come soon to get me.

Carol sits beside me. "Mom, I'll talk to the nurse and make sure it's okay for you to go shopping. You can make bouquets another time. *Please?* I woke up before dawn to catch a commuter flight from Toronto to Ottawa so I could get here in time. I've been looking forward to spending the day with you." She takes my hand in hers. "Will you come with me?"

I pull away. Who does she think she is, just showing up here and expecting me to jump? I already have plans.

She steps backward, sits on the bed, shifts her eyes toward the floor. A hot wave surges through me. Here is my daughter wanting to spend time with me, and I'm trying to brush her off. When did I turn into my own mother, the person I swore I wouldn't be? That horror I always felt when Mother made it clear I didn't matter—here I am doing the same to Carol.

"Of course, I'll go with you," I tell her. I tug at my wristband. "The thing is I don't have any money to go shopping."

"Mom, you don't have to worry about money. I will pay for whatever you need and get it later from your bank account. Remember?"

"I don't want you to pay. I want my own money. I'm not a child."

"It's the same thing. It *is* your money. It's just that you can't keep cash here. We keep it in the bank so it doesn't get lost or stolen. We've gone over this so many times."

"Have we?" I say.

Carol softens. "I'm sorry. Let's start over. Will you come shopping with me?"

I open my closet and pull a purse down from the top shelf. It's empty. I slide open a drawer and choose a pen, a small notepad, some tissues, and lipstick, tuck them into the purse, and snap it shut. I slip in a chocolate bar from the stash I keep hidden too, just in case we get hungry.

"Okay. Let's go."

The elevator beeps and refuses to move.

"You need the secret code," I say.

Carol ducks out, speaks to a uniform and returns quickly. "You're right, we need a code," she says as she punches in the numbers, discreetly shielding them with the palm of her hand.

"Don't worry," I assure her, "I wouldn't remember it anyway."

She puts her arm around my shoulder. "What should we do first? Do you want to look at shoes before you get too tired?"

"Sure."

Carol had parked the rental car in the loading zone just outside the door. As we drive away, I think about the plan that Audrey and I have been forming. What type of shoes would be best for wearing on our vacation? "Could I get running shoes?" I ask.

"Running shoes! Why would you want those?"

"Sometimes we do exercises. I've been thinking that they would be better for walking around the halls too—you know—give me support."

Carol laughs. "Okay, if that's what you want, we'll look for running shoes but not ones with too much tread. They might stick to the carpet, and you know falls can be very dangerous at your age. Your bones are brittle."

Hah! We're off to a good start. We drive through the downtown. I watch as buildings whiz past, trying my best to take in all the storefronts, amazed at never having been on this main street before. We pass a large bank that looks vaguely familiar.

"Is that my bank?" I ask.

"No, Mom. You always dealt with People's Bank. It's near here though."

"Can we drive by it?" I ask, trying to sound casual.

I dig in my purse and pull out the pen and notepad. I scratch the words *People's Bank* on the first page and wait.

"What are you writing?" Carol asks.

"Just jotting down a few notes, Dear. I find it useful to write things down. My memory's not that good these days."

Carol turns right and eases down the busy street. "There's the bank you always dealt with. Remember?"

I look out the window, then back to my pen and paper. "What street is this?"

"Albert Street. That should be easy to remember— Dad's name."

"Bless his soul. Is it really Albert Street?"

"Yep."

"Good." I write down *Albert Street*. "And do I still have an account there?"

"Yes Mom, we didn't change it. We do all your banking online now, so it doesn't really matter where the physical bank is."

I bite my lip. "I'm going to need some money. Can we go

in and get some?" I look directly at Carol and watch as her eyes make a slight rolling motion before she catches herself.

"Okay. Sure, we'll go in and you can take out twenty dollars. You're right. You should be able to carry some money with you."

Inside, Carol pulls out a card with the bank name and some numbers on it and shows it to me. "You should have one of these in your wallet. Did you bring it?"

I don't recognize it at all.

"You need it to access your account." Carol swipes the card and taps in some numbers. "Your password is your birthday, February 26. 0-2-2-6. There you go, now tell the woman what you want."

"I'll take five hundred dollars please," I say.

The teller's eyes shift focus to where Carol is standing just behind me, and then she nods slightly.

"I can only give you twenty dollars right now, Mrs. Gorsen. Is that okay?"

"Well, I haven't been shopping in quite some time but it seems to me I'll have a hard time finding shoes for under twenty dollars. Wouldn't you agree, Carol?" I ask, turning to see her expression.

"Maybe fifty would be better," she says, nodding to the teller.

"Fine, fine," I say, rubbing the bills between my thumb and forefinger and tucking them into my purse. "Thank you, Dear."

Just inside the air-conditioned mall, Carol gets a squirmy look on her face, like she wants to ask me something but knows she shouldn't.

"What is it, Dear?"

"They have wheelchairs here for customers' use. Do you want me to get one? It's a long walk from one end to the other."

"Well," I say, "I'm not sure I can push you all that way, but you can get one if you like."

She laughs. "Touché."

The shoe store clerk is very indifferent, interested only in flirting with two young boys who are skulking around near the ball cap display.

"Barbara," I call to the girl. "Barbara." The clerk continues to ignore me.

"Who are you talking to?" Carol asks.

"The salesgirl. It's Barbara. You know—my friend Trudy's daughter."

Carol shakes her head. "No, Mom. Barbara's much older now, older than me. That's not Barbara."

"Yes it is. Why must you always try to correct me?"

I wave my arm in the air to get the girl's attention.

She finally tears herself away from her admirers and strolls over to help us. "Can I find a size for you?"

"Yes. I'd like to try that shoe," I say, pointing at a colorful running shoe on the shelf. "I take a size eight, Barbara."

The girl shoots me a puzzled look and returns a few minutes later with a box, drops it on the chair beside me, and turns her attention back to the boys. Carol helps me lace the shoes.

"She's become quite rude," I say loudly to Carol, not caring if the girl hears. "Trudy would tan her hide if she saw the way she's acting."

I walk around the store, head down, admiring the blue

and yellow firmness and support. "I like these. They make me feel young. I want these."

Carol waits in line to pay. On the wall, I spy backpacks.

"Carol, I believe I need a bag too."

She steps out of line and sits down beside me. "What could you possibly need a backpack for?" she asks. Her voice is now ever-so-slightly edged with impatience.

"Because I've never had one, and I want one."

"But why? Why would you want one?"

I raise my eyebrows and say nothing.

Carol walks toward the bags. "Which one do you like?"

I point to a small, navy pack with peacock blue pockets and zippers. She plucks it from the display and pays for it along with the shoes. I grin. I can't help myself. I'm very pleased with having thought of it. It will surely come in handy on our vacation.

We shop a bit longer, then leave the mall and drive back into the city to a restaurant in Byward Market Square. Carol reminds me we used to meet here for lunch. It's now a bistro, she points out, run by a co-operative. Young and middle-aged folks talk on cell phones or read laptop screens, anything, it seems, except talk to one another. The menu, chalked on the wall in pink, yellow, green, and blue, lists mostly items that I don't recognize, though Carol is kind enough to explain that they're made with healthy grains and berries, fruit and cheese from places I've never been.

"I'll just have a bowl of soup," I say.

I take out my notebook and add *shoes* and *backpack* right below the name of the bank. And *money*. I write that too.

We order cups of something called fair-trade, organic

coffee and carry them outside to sit in the shade of a small maple tree.

"Mom, how are you? How are things at Tranquil Meadows?"

How am I? How are things? I've never really stopped to consider these questions, or at least not to answer them out loud. "It's fine there, I guess. They're good to me most of the time...."

Carol's expression is much softer than I usually picture it. She looks like she's trying to understand.

"I'm lonely," I admit. "I miss you and your brother and my friends. I wish Albert was still with us. And everything is timed, you know, like a timetable. I eat when they tell me, sleep when they tell me, play bingo when they tell me. Jeez, I even have a poop when they tell me. I could never poop on demand before. I don't know why I have to start now. And my back hurts all the time."

"You're being a good sport about all of this. I know it's not what you and Dad would choose, if he were still alive. I wish I lived closer and could visit you more, but I really have to be in Toronto with my job right now. At least I know you're being well cared for."

Back to the same thing she always says. I know it and so does she.

"It's okay. I know you and Tom were thinking of my well-being when you put me in The Home." Sometimes it's hard to resist playing the martyr card.

"It sounds awful when you call it *The Home*," Carol says, "like we've committed you to a locked psych ward from some bygone era."

I empty my cup. "Delicious coffee," I say. "Now, you

should take me back to *The Home* so you can be on your way. We've had a good day."

At supper, Audrey looks relieved to see me. "Where did you go?" she asks.

"I'm sorry I didn't have a chance to tell you. Carol came and took me shopping. Did you go to the craft class?"

Audrey nods. "It was good. We made things with dried-out weeds and glue."

I touch her hand and spot the white and blue bracelet still wrapped securely around her wrist, just under the cuff of her shirt.

Days blur together. I suffocate beneath a heavy woolen canopy suspended too close to my face. The invisible shroud makes it hard to breathe. I stay in bed. People come and go. They try to convince me to get up, to eat something, to have a bath. I don't know who they are and tell them all to go to hell. But they won't. They just keep coming.

My mother is here and my granny. At first, Mother is apologetic for missing the interview she set up with my teacher, for forgetting the gift for my friend Helen's birthday party, but it doesn't take long till she starts to ignore me, talking to Gran as if I'm not here and going on about that stupid man she married after Dad died. He doesn't come. Just as well. He's a nasty waste of space.

Albert sits on my bed and stays for a long time, though everyone else ignores him. I tell him I love him, then I hit him and tell him to leave. It's his fault that I'm in this awful place. We should be together. It's not fair that I am here alone and he is at home in his recliner, reading the paper and doing the crossword and visiting the kids without me. Damn it! I say goodnight to him every night before I go to sleep. He isn't here, but I know he can hear me.

I get up to use the bathroom, but when I do, the lady in the next bed pounds on the door and tells me to get out—that she needs to go. After that, I just pee the bed.

It's morning. Laughter outside my room and a uniform's cold hand on my arm wake me to a sense of overwhelming hunger. In my closet, I find a new pair of running shoes and a pretty blue backpack. I close the door, then open it and look again. These are my shirts and pants. This is my room, my quilt. I dress and try on the shoes—a perfect fit. I tie them and walk down the hall in search of the dining room.

"How are you feeling today, Lillian?" someone asks as I pass by the desk.

"I'm fine, Dear."

She smiles. "I can see that."

She says something quietly to the other girl behind the desk, and the two of them laugh.

"I'm sorry. Did you say something, Dear?" I ask.

"No, just glad you're feeling better. You had a couple of rough days. It's good to have you back."

My doctor has told me I'll have good days and bad, and I know he's right. People tell me stories about things I say and do; things I don't remember at all. I don't always believe them. I call these my fog days. I try to let them go. Thinking about them too much makes my stomach and head hurt.

I take my seat at the table, happy to join Eleanor, the

little girl, and Audrey for breakfast. They show no signs of missing me.

"What are we doing today?" I ask. "Does anyone know?" Eleanor delivers a flurry of beautiful phrases followed by a smile. The frizzy-haired girl giggles, and Audrey, between bites of toast, suggests in a hushed voice that today would be a good day to ditch the fancy watches.

She mimes a driver, arms steering wildly out in front, stopping to lean on the horn in the center of the imaginary steering wheel. "Vacation?" she hints.

3

"AAAH." I WINK AT AUDREY and wave to the coach standing in the doorway. I call her Coach because she's forever trying to get us to play, to be a team, to mingle. Also, I can't remember her name.

I pretend to be interested in the plan for the day. "What are we making today? I hope it's something kinky with paper and glue and scissors. I feel very creative this morning."

She laughs. I can tell she likes me. She always makes a special effort to include me, even though, I have to admit, I'm not very cooperative when it comes to being herded around in a group, doing what everyone else is doing.

"Well, my friend Lillian, we could make centerpieces for the birthday party next week. How does that sound?"

"Perfect. Audrey wants to help too."

The woman narrows her eyes and cocks her head playfully. "What are you two up to?"

"Nothing, we're just looking for something to fill our time," I say, blushing and trying to cover it by wiping my mouth with my napkin.

"Okay. I'll be back at ten to take you downstairs and we'll create magnificent table decorations. See you then."

I wander back in search of my room. There's a wonderful spring in each step with my new shoes. In the elevator, on our way to the activity room, the alarm chimes before the uniform enters the code, then we drop to the floor below.

The coach—is it Kathy, Karen, Sharon?—has gathered a hodgepodge of ribbon and flowers and decorating bits. In the middle of the table sits a bottle of glue and a colossal pair of scissors.

"Well, ladies, you can get started with what's here, and if you need anything else, just give me a shout. I'll be doing some paperwork at that table," she says, pointing across the room.

"Thank you, Dear," I say. "We'll see what we can do."

We set to work, poking stems into the sponges and setting them in the pots. I pick up the scissors and snip a piece of ribbon from the roll. Sharp! Excellent! I reach for Audrey's hand, carefully slip one blade under the band and squeeze. The SafeChip falls quietly onto the table. My pulse speeds up. I hand the scissors to Audrey and hold out my arm. *Snip.* I drop the bracelet into my pocket and direct Audrey to do the same, then tug at my sleeve to be sure it extends fully over my wrist.

We finish the centerpieces, careful to use all the flowers and ribbon, then sit back to admire our handiwork. I used to do these sorts of things with my Aunt Fraise when I was younger. She always tried to keep me busy making something. She was good at it too. She taught me how to embroider and crochet. She even bought me the wool and helped me make an afghan for my sister. She loved it. Come to think of it, Fraise was probably the one who made that green and purple blanket on my bed!

"All done?" Coach asks.

"Yep. How do they look?"

"Lovely. Thank you for your help. I may just put you two in charge of table decorations every month now that I see how talented you are."

Back in the elevator with our chaperone, the alarm begins to chime. Audrey reaches for her wrist, a confused look on her face.

I pat her pocket and lock eyes with her. "Shh," I say.

"What's that Lillian?" the woman asks as she punches in the code. "Did you say something?"

I shake my head and look innocent.

Back on the floor, I gesture for Audrey to follow me. I show her the backpack. "Isn't it great? Look at all the zippers. Do you have a bag to put your things in for our trip?" I ask.

"It's at home. I'm not sure where though; maybe in the attic." Audrey says. "Have you thought about where we should go?"

"What if we just go nowhere in particular—just go?"

"Sounds risky," Audrey says.

"Now you're talking! We're in it for the adventure, right? It doesn't really matter as long as we go somewhere."

I find my notebook and search for the list. At the bottom, I add *wristbands gone*. "We're doing great!" I say. "We have car keys," I add that to the list. "New shoes and a backpack for me, a big purse for you, some money, the address of my bank so we can get more money, and the wristbands are gone. It's coming together."

I'm feeling very proud, almost cocky about this clarity. I do know that it isn't always so. It's like I'm back. It gives me promise.

"Let's eat lunch, and then we can pack our clothes." I say.

On our way to the table, we stop to look out the window. We're not allowed outside much—never, in fact, unless we're on the special bus for some sort of goofy outing. I don't mean goofy, really. The market is fun, but we don't get to take money so we can only look. And we get ice cream on our way back. That's good. I miss the outdoors though. I can sit for hours and look out the window like I'm watching TV or something.

A blue taxi is parked out front. The driver opens the passenger door to let someone in. On the side, painted in large white figures, there is a phone number. I pull a pen from my pocket and a napkin from the table and write it down.

Audrey is watching. "Do you always keep a pen in your pocket?"

"Yeah. You never know when you'll need to remember something." I replace the pen and tuck the napkin in beside it, poking around and pulling out a wrinkled message from a few days ago. "Good things happen when you write them down," I say. "Don't worry. Everything will work out. It always does."

I stab my fork into the crusty topping on the macaroni and cheese, one of my favorite lunchtime dishes. I raise it to my mouth but it's hard to swallow. I manage a few bites and a cup of weak coffee, then slurp down some half-melted orange sherbet.

Back in my room, I fold pants and shirts, nightgowns, underwear and socks into my pack, then take them out and put them back again. Every article of clothing has a big white tag stitched on it with my name—even socks and bras. I can't figure out how it is that my clothes are always getting stolen right out of my closet when they're marked so clearly. No one believes me. They say the missing clothes are in the laundry, or that I never had red pajamas. But I've seen other people wearing my clothes. I have.

Despite my bravado with Audrey, I'm unsure about leaving. I can't decide what to bring, what to leave behind. Tranquil Meadows is suddenly very comfortable and secure. I finally hide the bag in the closet and lie on the bed to rest, my back throbbing and my mind numb.

I stare at my supper. I have trouble concentrating.

Audrey leans close. "Are you packed?"

"Yes, I'm ready. What about you?"

"I found a big shopping bag in my closet and filled it with clothes, pajamas, and soap and things," Audrey says. "I even stuffed two rolls of toilet paper in the bottom just in case. And I emptied my purse again to be sure the keys and money were still there and found a credit card, not yet expired. That might be useful too." She can hardly contain her excitement. "This is gonna be great."

"Wonderful," I say, trying to gather some enthusiasm.

"What's wrong? Are you having nerves?" Audrey asks.

"No, no. I'm just a little tired. I want to go. For sure. I'll feel better tomorrow." I pick at my food. My stomach is telling me to stay, but a stronger sense somewhere inside is urging me to get away from this sameness of one day to the next.

Daylight nudges under the curtain that surrounds my bed. At first I have only a vague sense that today is special, but when I rise and open my closet, I spy the backpack, brightly colored and filled with all my things. My heart starts to race. I dress as quickly as I can, my muscles and joints creaking and moaning, tie my running shoes, and leave my room in search of the dining room. The route is short and surprisingly direct.

The air conditioner billows clouds of icy air into the room. I don't like the cold. Inside this place, I'm always wrapped in a sweater. The idea of driving along a hot country road with my bare arm out the open window makes me smile.

"Good morning," I say, joining Audrey at the window.

"It sure is." Audrey waves her arm toward the sky. "Look at that beautiful...ocean. Not a cloud in sight. How are you this morning?" she asks.

"Fit as a fiddle. And you?"

"A little nervous."

I try to reassure her. "It'll be an adventure—no expectations. We'll be like Jack Whatsisname. You know, *On the Road*? Or Bob Hope and Bing Crosby in *The Road to...*wherever? We'll just see where we end up."

Porridge, toast, scrambled eggs. We leave the dining hall and arrive first at my room. "Come in for a minute," I say. "We need to decide how this is going to work."

Audrey looks confused. "I thought we'd decided that."

"But the details—we need to talk about the details, like

where is your car. And a letter—we should leave a letter explaining that we're fine so they don't worry."

"Right," Audrey agrees without much thought.

We compose a letter on a small sheet of paper from the pad in my purse, then tuck it under the pillow with a corner peeking out. I gather my purse and backpack, struggling to maneuver the pack over the hump on my back—a dowager's hump. Such an ugly name. My doctor has explained that it was caused by long-term damage from advanced something-or-other-osis. I don't usually notice it's there unless I happen to catch sight of it in a window or mirror. Audrey tries to help me get the pack on properly but the straps are too short. I finally sling both straps over my right shoulder.

I poke my head out the doorway. "The hall's empty. Everyone must still be eating. Let's go to your room."

I motion to Audrey to walk behind me. Turning in the opposite direction from the workstation, we walk single file around the rectangle to Audrey's room. Quickly ducking sideways into the room, I breathe a deep sigh. "We made it this far. Your room is perfect. We can see the elevators and the desk from here. Is your car in the parking lot?"

"Maybe. No. I don't have a car."

"The one you sold to the boy. Where is it?"

"Probably parked at his house, I guess. They live next door."

"To here?" I ask.

"No...to my house."

"Then we'll need a taxi. Do you have a phone?"

Audrey looks around. "My roommate does."

I wave the phone number in the air. "I need to call the cab. Do you have your bags ready?"

Audrey pulls the large shopping bag and purse from her closet. "I just have to go to the bathroom, and then we can go. Don't call until I come out."

The room is dark and turquoise. Heavy cotton drapes hang ready to circle each bed, the same drab color as the ones in my room. They make me think of a stifling tent and of how glad I am to be leaving.

The bathroom door opens and Audrey steps out with an armful of Depends adult diapers in the shape of underwear. "We'll need these. I almost forgot. When you're traveling there isn't always a bathroom close by. That could be bad."

"Good thinking," I say. "Have you got room in your bag? Here, give me some." I swing my backpack around and lay it on the bed. Just as I zip it up, a face pokes through the doorway.

"Oh good, I've caught you both in one place. We're heading down in half an hour to hear a choir sing oldies but goodies. Will you join us?"

I move to stand in front of my pack. "Not today, Dear," I reply.

"No? What about you Audrey?"

"No, I don't think so," she says. "I've got a few things to do here."

The woman continues down the hall, recruiting an audience.

I take the napkin from my pocket and check back over my shoulder. "You watch the door while I phone the taxi." I dial and wait. "Hello? Could you please send a car to Tranquil Meadows Nursing Home to pick up two passengers? We'll be waiting outside...Pardon? Where do we want to go? Could you wait for a minute please?" I hold my hand over the receiver. "What's your address?" I ask Audrey.

She stares blankly back at me. "I don't know."

"Just downtown," I tell the man. "Thank you."

I hang up the phone and clap my hands. "Come on, my friend. We're getting out of here." As I slip the number back into my pocket, my fingers stumble on something hard. "Oh, wait. I still have the wristband in here." I drop it onto Audrey's bedside table.

In the hallway, I reach for the button and the elevator doors open. From inside, a stranger peers out. "Is this the upper floor?" he asks.

Audrey nearly bursts into tears. "Yes—upper floor—yes!" she blurts.

She squeezes past him, bags and cane crashing against the frame, into the elevator.

I step back to let the man out, and, with a quick glance up and down the hallway, step inside. I push the button to close the door.

"Oh, my Lord," Audrey says, breaking into laughter. "He scared the bejeezus out of me. I thought he was a doctor."

The hall is empty on the ground floor and the daylight shines from just around the corner, encouraging us on. We walk slowly and deliberately down the hall, toward the double doors leading outside.

"Oh no!" I say, as my shoulder mashes against the door. "It's locked."

Audrey drags her bag along the floor like it was a dead weight. Cane, step, drag, cane, step, drag. She points to the doorframe where there is another keypad. Stooped and silent, we stare out through the glass.

A blue taxi pulls up out front. A man gets out and comes

to the door. He pushes a button outside and the lock releases.

"Hello, ladies. Are you the two who called for a cab?"

"That's us." I turn to Audrey and wink. "Isn't this our lucky day?"

The man opens the car door and helps us in, then stores our bags in the trunk.

Part II

Fly

The Vacation

4

"WHERE TO, LADIES?"

Audrey clutches her purse and snaps open the latch. She leafs through the items inside until she finds her wallet, and inside that, her license. Probably expired long ago, it still has her house address on it. She reads it to the driver.

"Okay. I know where that is," he says, pulling away from the curb.

We ride for what seems like forever through the streets of Ottawa, my head spinning as I try to recognize the city I've lived in all of my life. Finally, we stop in front of a white clapboard house, dressed up with shutters and a porch across the front and one side. It seems out of place with the others on the street. They're a little rundown and tired, in need of some paint.

"This is the place," the driver says. "I'll help you with your bags." He sets the shopping bag and backpack on the sidewalk and opens the door, offering a hand to Audrey. I ease out on my own.

"Can I help you carry your things?" the man asks.

"Oh no, we're fine. Thank you, young man." Audrey bats her eyelashes and flashes a wrinkled smile.

She's always flirting with men—all men. It doesn't matter whether they're young, old, filthy, or well groomed.

He forces a polite smile. "That'll be eighteen dollars then," he says.

Audrey hands the man a twenty-dollar bill. "Thank you for your help."

As the cab pulls away, I scan the street. "So this is where you lived? Nice neighborhood."

Audrey looks again at the house. I can't read anything from her expression. She seems almost curious, questioning if this is the place.

"Someone else is living here. I wonder where Terry is. Those curtains are flowered—ours are beige—and there's a bicycle on the veranda. I've never seen that before."

"So, where do you think your car might be?" I ask. "Did you say the boy next door bought it?"

"I think so. He lives there," Audrey says, pointing to the house on the right. "Or is it the one next to that? Let me think. I don't remember exactly. I don't really know my neighbors that well. Terry doesn't like me to be too friendly. He always says people are nosey—they don't need to know our business. I think the neighbor kids are kind of afraid of him because on Halloween, I watch them go right past our house if they see his car in the driveway, and I notice that the newspaper girl only collects when he isn't home."

We set our bags down and walk a short distance along the street. The car is nowhere to be found.

"Good grief. Here we are, packed and ready to go on vacation, keys in hand, and we can't find the car. Are you sure the boy even lived around here?"

"Yes. It's got to be here somewhere." She turns around a little too quickly, loses her balance, and whacks me on the ankle with her cane.

I shake it off. "I'm fine. Let's just keep looking for the car. What color is it again?"

"Blue, a blue Oldsmobile Intrigue," Audrey says. "I know that because I used to repeat it to myself over and over when I was in the mall so I'd be able to find it when I went out to the parking lot."

"I understand, believe me. Now, where could this blue Intrigue be hiding? Maybe it's in a garage. You scoot up there and have a look through the window. I'll wait here."

Audrey turns around, horrified. "I can't do that. What if someone sees me?"

She looks up and down the street and her face brightens. She points across the road. "There it is—my car! The boy lives across the street. Now I remember."

"Halleluiah! Come on, we're off then."

The key fits right into the lock like magic. We stash our bags in the backseat and I take my place behind the wheel.

"I can't remember the last time I drove. Let me see now…"

I look for the lights on the left of the steering column— bright—dim—off; another knob on the right squirts water onto the windshield. I feel under the seat for the lever so my feet can reach the pedals and adjust the rearview mirror.

Finally, I turn the key in the ignition. The car fills with a thunderous roar as music blasts from the speakers.

"Heaven help us!" Audrey shouts. "That scared me."

We fumble with knobs on the dashboard, looking for the volume button. Audrey pushes one that starts a fan blowing full-speed. Eardrums pulsing and hair flying in the gale-force winds, we sit back and howl with laughter.

Once we have the buttons and knobs figured out, I shift into reverse. The car rolls slowly backward onto the street. I sit very straight, my nose inches from the steering wheel, turn the wheel, and accelerate cautiously.

"This is a cinch." We cruise down the block and around the corner. "We need money," I say. "Any idea where the bank is?"

Audrey stares blankly ahead.

"Can you check my purse? I might have written it down."

She finds my notebook and leafs through the pages. She looks up just in time to shout, "Stop sign!"

I slam on the brakes, screeching to a halt in the middle of the intersection. A car approaching from the right slows to a stop and the driver waves a little too vigorously, motioning us to move out of the way.

"Oh dear! You'll have to help me watch for signs," I say. "I'm out of practice."

Audrey stays pretty calm. "It's okay. No harm done. Just pull over up here, and we'll talk about where we're going."

The car rolls to the curb, and Audrey shows me the notebook. "Is this it? People's Bank, Albert Street?"

"Yeah, that's it. Do you know where that is?"

"Not really. I have a hunch the downtown is this way,"

Audrey says, pointing to the right. "It looks more squishy in that direction, more tall buildings all mashed together."

"Okay, off we go then," I say, touching the gas pedal and pulling back onto the road.

A red van swerves around the front end of the Intrigue, horn blasting.

"Jeez Louise! I thought I checked the side mirror."

Audrey's breathing sounds heavy, as if she's struggling to get oxygen. "Maybe this driving isn't such a good idea."

"Nonsense, it was just a miscalculation. That bus came out of nowhere." I turn at the next corner onto a busier street.

Audrey sits straight, her head swiveling left, right, to the front and back, calling out traffic signals and signs as we approach each intersection.

I am silent, concentrating hard.

"Albert Street!" I shout, as the sign comes into view at the last minute. I veer to the right, round the corner, and almost hit a man who jumps out of the way with, as near as I can tell, a few choice words sent in my direction.

"Good grief, you need to give more warning!" Audrey says.

Trying to forget about the close call, I drive on. Two blocks later, Audrey spots the bank's sign. There is an empty parking space right in front. I edge slowly up beside the car that's there, point the front end toward the curb and inch in. The front wheel hits the curb. Two drivers honk and pull out around us, shaking their heads as they pass. So rude and impatient! I put the car in reverse and back out, pull forward beside the car in front and try to back in. It's hard to turn that far around. This time the back wheel hits the curb, the front, stubbornly street-bound.

Audrey's looking out the side window at a young man watching us from a bench in front of the bank. She smiles.

"This is hard," I say. "The space is too small." I try to catch my breath, which I hadn't even noticed I'd been holding. I could just leave the car this way. I'm sure I won't be long in the bank, but traffic has already started to gather behind us.

Audrey glances again at the young man on the bench and back at me. I see the look in her eye. Lord have mercy! The world does not need an eighty-year-old flirt. She rolls down the window. "Excuse me, Handsome. Could you help us, Dear?" she asks. "We're having a little trouble."

He answers from his place on the bench. "What's up?"

I shout past Audrey before she has a chance to speak again. "Do you drive?"

"Yep."

"Could you possibly park this thing while I run into the bank? I've left my glasses at home and I'm having a little problem judging."

The boy looks amused. He shrugs his shoulders and sidles over to the car. "Yeah. No problem."

"Thank you. I'll just be a few minutes. Audrey will wait in the car."

Audrey looks pleased.

"You behave, now," I say, patting her on the knee. I struggle out of the car and wave to the drivers lined up behind. "Thank you, young man."

I turn to watch as he wheels the car out, then smoothly, accurately, maneuvers it into position next to the curb.

The bank is mostly empty, but I make my way through the hallway of plush, velvet handrails that lead to the teller's window and stand in front of a surly looking young woman who barely acknowledges my presence. She continues to slot paper-clipped bundles into a drawer and write letters and numbers on bits of paper.

"Excuse me," I say.

"I'll be right with you, Ma'am."

I hate being called Ma'am. It sounds so condescending, like I'm some sort of old babe who doesn't understand how busy and important others are with their whole busy and important lives ahead of them.

I wait as patiently as I can. Finally she looks up. "Can I help you?"

"I'd like to take out some money, please."

"Okay. Just swipe your card right there and enter your PIN," she says, pointing to a keypad on the counter.

"I'm not sure what you mean. I just want to take money out of my account. I'd like five hundred dollars, please."

She examines me with a curious look. "What's your name?"

"Lillian Gorsen. I've had an account here for more than fifty years, and I'll thank you to respect that. I'd like to withdraw one thousand dollars."

The girl taps some information into her computer and reads the screen. "Do you have any photo ID?" she asks.

"What? For crying out loud," I say. I sift through my purse and pull out my health card. "Will this work?"

"One minute please, Mrs. Gorsen." She closes and locks her drawer as if I am going to reach across and steal the money while she's gone. She hurries around the end of the counter into an office and closes the door behind her. A moment later, she returns with an older gentleman, older than her at least. He shakes my hand politely and greets me like a long lost friend.

"Mrs. Gorsen, how are you? It's been ages. I miss seeing Albert in here. He always had a good story and a ready laugh."

I don't have a clue who this man is, but I play along. "Thank you. I'm happy to see you again. My dear Albert was indeed a gem. So kind of you to say so. Now, is there a problem with my account?"

"No. Everything is in order. It's just that your children have power of attorney on this account and most of the transactions lately have been done through them. Your name remains on the paperwork as well though, so you do have access to the money. That's not a problem."

"Excellent. Thank you."

"Are you going on a trip or making a big purchase, Lillian?" he asks nonchalantly.

"I'm buying gifts for Tom and Carol. That's why I want to get the money out myself. I want to surprise them. You won't tell them, will you?" The lies spill from my mouth, unrehearsed. I watch him closely to see what he will do.

"It's our secret then. Nice to see you again and know that you're keeping well, Lillian. Have a great day." He shakes my hand once more, gives a quick nod to the teller, and returns to his office. The young lady counts out the bills, and I tuck them into my purse.

Outside, I sit down on the bench and try to breathe deeply.

Audrey looks up from her discussion with her new friend. "I was just having a nice chat with Wayne," she says, then quietly adds, "he's homeless."

"Wayne? Does your family live in Ottawa?" I ask. There

is a sleeping bag, an enormous backpack, and a guitar case piled at the end of the bench.

"It's Rayne," he says, looking a little annoyed, "like the wet stuff that falls from the sky. My dad lives in Squamish, B.C. I sort of travel around to wherever there's work. I'm a musician."

"He's a great driver too. Did you see how well he parked the car?" Audrey says. "He's really a nice guy, Lillian. He's trying to save enough money to get back to British Columbia so he can see his dad again." Audrey cups her hand over the side of her mouth and whispers, "His girlfriend just left him, and he can't afford to keep the apartment where they lived."

She pats his hand. "I'm so sorry to hear you're down on your luck. Here, let me give you something for your kindness." She reaches into her purse, pulls out a twenty-dollar bill and hands it to him.

"Does your father know your situation?" I ask.

Rayne tucks the bill in his pocket. "Yeah, not that it's any of your business." He looks up again with a sheepish look, like he feels a little guilty for talking to me that way. "I can go home as long as I find a job."

He pulls a pack of cigarettes from his shirt and lights one. The smoke streams straight up as he exhales in the dead heat of the city street. The stillness of the air around us bakes my skin, seeps into my scalp, feels so good.

I watch him inhale, watch his yellowed finger twitch slightly. His skin is sallow, and his eyes are rimmed with dark shadows. Still, he has a boyish look; a look of innocence, like my son, Tom.

Tom—always so evasive with us. Always leaving, always hiding from everything that meant being part of our family. Even when he was a young boy.

"Tom, you should come home. It's time you took on some responsibility and got a job. You and Carol are all we have—all *I* have now that your father's gone. That fellow in the bank was just saying what a good man Albert was, how kind and funny. Do you remember how he was the only one who could make you laugh?"

Tom looks blankly at me and then at Audrey.

"He was always on your side. I'd get so angry with you for not coming home, not phoning, taking the car without telling us, skipping school. He always supported you. You should come home—and you should give up those damned cigarettes."

Audrey takes my hand. "Lillian, this isn't Tom. This is Rayne."

"Tom, Rayne. It doesn't matter what he calls himself. We named him Thomas and I will continue to call him that. Tom for short."

Audrey stands and balances with her cane to help pull me up too. "Let's go," she says. "This vacation isn't going to plan itself." She turns to Tom and shakes his hand. "Thanks for your help. Good luck getting home."

The young man shakes our hands. "Good luck to you too," he says.

"Are you sure you won't come home with us?" I ask. "Carol would be happy to see you."

"No. No, I'm just gonna stay here," he says.

I can't stand the lost look on his face. I just want to give him a huge hug. It's as if he doesn't even recognize me. I stand for a moment and watch him return to his place on the bench.

He was so different from Carol right from the beginning. Such a quiet baby. He hardly cried. Just amused himself,

content with things. Carol—now she was another story alto-
gether—demanding and impatient, always wanting more.
She wanted figure skating lessons, then piano lessons, singing lessons, and she even tried to convince us she needed to
go to a private school. And me a teacher in a public school!
That wouldn't have been right. When Tom was a teenager, he
never argued, just ran away from everything. Nothing mat-
tered enough to cause a fuss.

I move to hug him, but he just stays seated, and I feel
him stiffen. Neither of us says a word. I know that I have to
let him go. He's a man after all, not my little boy.

Behind the wheel, I pull slowly, easily away from the
curb, thanks to the empty parking space now in front of us.
I drive around the block just to get used to stopping and
turning. As we pass the bank again, Audrey waves and reaches
across to honk the horn.

"Stop it," I tell her. "You're gonna make me get in an
accident. I can't drive with you grabbing the steering wheel
like that. Jeez!" She can be so aggravating sometimes, making herself so popular with my son. It isn't fair, and now she's
tormenting me by honking while I'm trying to drive.

"Sorry," Audrey says. "Where are we going, anyway?"

A space opens up on a side street and I pull over to park.
"I don't know. Didn't we have a plan? I don't know how
to get out of the city, do you? We can't just keep driving
around the block."

We sit there for hours, or maybe just minutes. Audrey
actually nods off, from the heat, I think. When she opens her
eyes, she starts right in with her crazy ideas about the boy.

"He wants to go out west, did you hear him say that? We

could go west," she says. "And you should see him handle the car—like a pro. And he has no place to stay here. Can we tell him he can come with us as long as he'll drive?"

"He's not a puppy, Audrey. We can't just take him along."

"He plays the guitar. He told me we remind him of his grandmother. He's a good boy. I just know it."

I'm surprised at how tired I feel. My arms are sore and my head is starting to ache. Driving through the city is like working on a puzzle, but not an easy jigsaw. It's more like one of those damned Sudoku puzzles. We are already lost, and it isn't even noon. "Okay. Let's go ask him, but we need to keep our wits. We don't really know him."

Audrey beams. "It's gonna be fine. I hope he's still there. Do you think you can find the bank?"

Rayne is sitting on the bench, smoking another cigarette when we circle around again. He is talking and laughing with some shady characters that look to be his age. There is no place to park this time so I just slow to a stop and Audrey rolls down the window.

"Excuse me," she hollers. "Rayne? Could you come here for a moment please?"

He jumps at the sound of his name and passes his cigarette to the girl sitting next to him. She takes a drag, then passes it on.

"That's not a cigarette," I say to Audrey. "They're smoking dope! Right on the street, if you please. This is not a good idea. I think we'd better just go."

"No, no. Let me talk to him," she insists.

"We have a proposition for you," Audrey says as he approaches the window. "You want to go out west, right? And it turns out, we want to go on a vacation out west as well, but we could use some help with the driving. What would you say about joining us? You drive and we'll do the rest."

He looks stunned. "Are you serious? You're heading to British Columbia?"

I lean over and point my finger toward the bench. "What is that you're smoking over there with your friends?"

"Tobacco." He glances back at the group. "Oh, yeah. You think it's pot because we're passing it around. No, we're just all poor, and we don't have many smokes left, so we're making them last. That's what we do."

"Uh-huh. That and a lot of other things from what I've heard. Now, we're gonna need to get this straight if you want to have a ride home. No illegal drugs allowed in this car. Do you understand?"

He starts to walk away. "Yeah, Grandma. I understand a little too well. You're starting to sound like my dad."

Audrey waves him back. "Does this mean you're not coming?" she asks. "I think it would work out for all of us. It would be fun."

He doesn't answer but returns to the bench with the others.

I'm getting fed up. "Let him go. He smokes marijuana, he has no job, and he clearly has an attitude. This was a bad idea."

Before I finish, Audrey is already out of the car. "I'm going to talk to him," she says.

The door hangs open, and traffic starts to build up behind me. I reach over with Audrey's cane and pull her door shut. That woman is so determined when she makes up her mind. I wave my hand out the window and drive slowly away. At the corner, I turn right and creep along. I can't make out the signs.

Cars whiz by. Everything looks sort of fuzzy.

In the middle of the block, I spot a large space. It is painted blue with a picture of a wheelchair and has lots of room to park. I head in, turn off the car, and start to cry.

A few minutes pass and my panic starts to fade. I'm such a fool sometimes. Where did I think I would go by myself? Audrey has to come with me. It wouldn't be any fun without her and besides, together we'll have better luck sorting things out.

I pick up her cane and start walking, hopefully in the right direction. I've been having trouble knowing which way is which in The Home, but I'm sure that's because everything always looks the same in there. That is definitely not the case here. It is all very new.

As I reach the corner, I can see a group of kids clustered around a bench. When I get closer, I see Audrey right in the middle of it all.

"Audrey," I say as I approach, "are you ready to go?"

Everyone turns to look at me.

"Where did you go?" Audrey asks.

"I parked around the corner. Are you coming?"

"I've convinced Rayne to come with us," she says. "He's going to drive. He knows the way."

Rayne looks at me. I look at him. We both look at Audrey.

She shrugs. "Well, let's go then. Grab your things."

Rayne heaves the gigantic pack over his shoulder and with guitar in one hand, sleeping bag in the other, says goodbye to his friends.

I walk ahead and Audrey follows. At the corner, I stop.

"Go right. I saw you turn that way," Rayne says.

"Very observant."

My legs are ready to crumple beneath me by the time we reach the car. Audrey is limping heavily on her bad leg. I hand the keys to Rayne, crawl into the back seat, and push our bags to one side. Rayne takes his place behind the wheel, Audrey, on the passenger side.

"Do you know how to get out of the city?" I ask.

"No problem."

"It's Lillian. You can call me Lillian."

"And Audrey," Audrey adds.

5

THE SCENERY IS CHANGING. We've left behind the tall buildings and sidewalks and are now on a highway, heading out of the city.

From the back seat, I watch Rayne's face reflected in the rearview mirror. He looks young, maybe twenty-five or -six, scruffy, hair too long, a sparse fringe of stubble poking randomly from his jaw.

"We have self-defense training, you know," I say.

He doesn't respond.

"We can protect ourselves in any circumstance. That cane is just a prop. Audrey doesn't really need it."

"Good," he says. "A couple of fossils like yourselves have to be careful traveling around on your own."

"I beg your pardon?" I sit up straighter in the seat. "Fossils? You've got a lot of nerve."

He laughs. "Relax, Lillian. I'm just setting up my own

rules for the trip. If we're gonna be traveling together, we need to be equals. No acting like my guardian, telling me what I can and can't do. You treat me with respect and I'll do the same for you. How's that sound?"

"But it's our car, and we're paying the way. You, young man, are our guest on this trip. And besides, we're older and wiser than you because we've had more life experience."

"Don't count on it, and besides, I have the keys to your car. That makes it mine in practical terms."

I feel queasy. This young tyrant is already taking over our car and has plans of his own. Audrey is being very quiet. She seems oblivious to the conversation. I lean forward to see what she's doing.

She has opened the glove compartment and is searching for something. She stops, reaches in, and pulls out a handful of flat, square plastic packages.

"What are these? Candies?" she asks. She looks more closely, turns them over, and squeezes them for clues, then reads the label. "Trojan Luscious Flavors Lubricated Condoms."

"Oh, good grief!" she shouts, dropping the packages in her lap. Her face flushes bright crimson. "These weren't here when this was my car." She gathers them up and stuffs them quickly to the back of the compartment.

"What do you mean 'when this *was* my car'?" Rayne asks.

"Well…this used to be my car, and then I sold it to the young boy next door. We're just borrowing it," Audrey says.

Rayne searches her face. "He knows you've borrowed it, right?"

A flash of heat surges through me. I'm feeling panicky, like we've forgotten something important. We should have left a note for the boy about that. Or did we?"

"Of course he knows! Of course. Otherwise it would be stealing." My words come out in a shrill pitch.

"Right," Rayne says quietly.

Audrey turns around. She doesn't add anything, just looks at me with a weird expression. I can't tell whether she is properly showing restraint or she just doesn't get what's going on.

She turns back to the front and smiles at Rayne. "You're a good driver."

My head is light, like it's floating above me, unattached. We've forgotten an important step; that much I know, but now I'll be dammed if I can remember what that piece is, or why it's important. It's gone. My hands busy themselves, fidget with the backpack on the seat beside me, open and close the zippers, and trace over and over the name on the front of the bag.

Rayne checks the rearview mirror. "You okay?"

"Yes. I'm very tired."

"Why don't you sleep? I know my way around. As long as we keep heading northwest, we're going in the right direction, and Audrey will wake you if we need you." He sounds sympathetic.

"No, I'd rather not," I say, struggling to stay focused. The face in the mirror and the kinder voice are Tom's. I relax and watch him. He's always kind, yet always a mystery to me. That first time he disappeared, he must have been twelve. He'd run away before but only to the next-door neighbor's or his best friend's house, and he'd always come back the same day. This time, no one knew where he was. I called everyone, even the police. They said they'd let the officers on the streets know, but it was too early to file a report—what's that called? What's that report when a child's missing and all the authorities are informed? Anyway, I must have called the police every name in the book when they said that. I took Carol and we walked up and down every street for blocks around, calling Tom's name and asking people if they'd seen him. Albert went looking for him in the car. After dark, I took Carol home and stayed up by the phone. No one called except Albert. He stayed out all night and kept stopping to check in with me. It was awful. Twelve years old. I couldn't imagine where he would be. The next day, the police finally came by the house after I called them again and yelled at them for not doing anything about my missing son. We were sitting at the table, looking through photographs to find a recent one, and in walked Tom, calm as you please. He'd spent the night in a fort that he'd built out of twigs or whatever, in a ravine a few blocks away because he was afraid he'd get scolded for some trouble he'd gotten into the day before at school. Unbelievable! We had no idea then that it would be a habit of his—refusing to take responsibility for his actions, running away. I still feel ill when I think of that day. I thought I was such a huge failure as a mom.

And now, here he is, taking us somewhere. Audrey seems to feel comfortable with him. She pulls a map from the glove compartment and unfolds it. It takes her a long time to find the spot but eventually her finger rests on the name, Ottawa, and a big smile crosses her face. "Here we are," she says.

Tom nods. He asks her quietly, probably thinking I can't hear, "Your friend…is she okay?"

"Mm-hmm, she's fine."

Leaving the city behind, we merge onto the main high-way going west. Traffic is heavy and fast. I'm dizzy watching the cars and trucks whiz by.

"Am I ever glad you're driving and not Lillian," Audrey says.

"Me too. That'd be disastrous," Tom says. He glances in the mirror and then tempers his comment a bit. "At least from what I saw with the parking situation."

"Oh, no. You're right," Audrey says. "Driving is more challenging at our age, no doubt about it, especially if you're out of practice."

"So, Lillian hasn't driven for a while?" Tom asks, obviously fishing for the story.

"No, we've been—Oh, look at that." She stops mid-sentence and points at a road sign showing restaurants and bathrooms ahead. "I could use a washroom break and a bite to eat. How about you?"

"Sure, I'll pull in."

The seatbelt gives me hard time and then the door handle. Everything is so complicated. Audrey and I meet in front of the car. Tom hangs back and follows behind. I slow and wait for him, so anxious to re-connect. I reach out to link arms with him and he freezes and gives me a strange look. Who is this? I snap my arm back and step ahead to catch up with Audrey.

"Who is that man?" I whisper.

"Rayne. That's Rayne. He's driving us out west."

"Do we know him?" I ask.

Audrey nods her head and pushes open the restroom door.

The fellow saunters toward the men's room, keys dangling from his hand.

"Excuse me," I say. "I need you to leave the car keys with me."

He hands them over without hesitation.

"Thank you."

I pull Audrey aside in the washroom and try to explain. "We need to be cautious. He makes me nervous, discombobulated."

"I trust him," Audrey answers. She ducks into a cubicle and shuts the door.

As I wash up, I'm surprised by the person I see in the mirror—so saggy and wrinkled, so pale.

"I feel peckish," Audrey says as we leave the washroom. "Can we sit down and have a sandwich and coffee?"

"Can we get you something, Rayne?" Audrey asks, as he joins us at the lunch counter.

The chairs are uncomfortable, all plastic and steel, but a welcome change from the heaviness of the ones at Tranquil Meadows. Who was it that always used to tell me 'a change is as good as a rest'? The newness of the situation will just take some getting used to.

I hand Rayne the keys as we walk back to the car.

"We're low on gas," he says. "We should fill up before we leave here."

When he finishes at the pump, he pops his head into the car, "Sixty-four dollars. We were almost on empty."

He takes the bills I offer and disappears inside.

We drive forever. Along the road, Audrey makes a game of reading the signs out loud, "Arnprior, Burnstown, Renfrew." She points at a sign for Algonquin Park.

"Lillian, did you ever go hiking there when you were a kid?"

"When my dad was alive, he used to take us hiking there, all seven of us. I loved it. After he died, and my mom married that dim-witted Stuart, we didn't go anywhere. Mom and Stuart seemed to get out often enough, but not the rest of us. We had to stay home and look after one another. You remember that, don't you Fraise?"

I look up and see Audrey. "I mean Audrey, sorry. I was thinking about my aunt, Fraise. I miss her so much.

"Later," I add, "when we were married, Albert and I used to take the kids camping and canoeing in Algonquin. He loved the wilderness. Maybe when we get back from our trip, I'll ask Albert if he wants to go camping there again."

Audrey's head has dropped back onto the headrest and she's purring. Rayne has stuffed white plugs in his ears with cords attached, like the ones I've seen the kids wearing as they walk past The Home on their way to and from school. I take up the work of reading the road signs so I'll know where we are.

At almost five o'clock, Highway 17 leads us into the small town of Mattawa. Rayne pulls into the parking lot of The Riverside Motel, an aging building on the outskirts of town.

"How does this look?" he asks.

"Looks like home," I say, "at least for tonight."

"I'll wait in the car," Rayne says as Audrey and I get out. I stand beside Rayne's window, anxious about leaving him there with the keys, but hesitant to ask for them again. I don't want to get into a contest at this point.

He opens the window and hands me the keys.

"Listen," he says. "I haven't really committed to this whole thing just yet. I'll let you know for sure in the morning.

I won't need a room here. I'll look after myself."

"You don't want a room?" I ask. "I didn't know you were undecided. When did you decide that you were undecided?" My legs are wobbly and I'm suddenly a child afraid that her parents are leaving and not coming back. "Where will you go?"

"Don't worry. I'll be fine. Can I just use the bathroom in your room to clean up?"

I nod, but this isn't making sense. "Why don't you stay? We'll pay for your room if that's what you're worried about. That's part of the deal."

"No," he says. "We don't exactly have a deal. We're working on a trial basis right now."

"Okay. Okay, you can use our bathroom. Maybe you can leave your things in our room too, for safekeeping. Then tomorrow night you'll probably change your mind and have a room of your own." I don't want to think about what he's going to do tonight or why he's saying these things.

A rustic wooden sign with *Office* burned into it hangs over the entrance. The screen door squeaks and then slams hard behind us. The smell of fried fish wafts from a back room and we can hear the clinking of silverware on a plate. A rather large man lumbers out to greet us.

"Hello, ladies. What can I do for you?"

"Do you have any available rooms for tonight?" I ask.

"You just need the one?"

"Yes, thank you. And just for tonight—we're only a passing fancy."

He gives me an odd look. "Number six is empty. It has two double beds."

FLEE, FLY, FLOWN

"Perfect. How much do you charge?"

The man glances out the window toward the car. "Just the two of you?" he asks, raising his bushy eyebrows high on his forehead.

"Just two," Audrey blurts out too abruptly.

"Hmmm. Sixty dollars. Checkout by eleven."

I pull the bills from my wallet and lay them on the counter.

The man, almost wedged between the counter and back wall, twists slowly and chooses a key from a nail on the pegboard behind him. He hands it to me and winks. "You have a g-o-o-d night now," he says, drawing out the words in a slimy drawl.

I slip the key ring over my finger. "Is there a restaurant you might recommend in town?"

"The diner on the main street, Mabel's, serves good home-cooked meals. That's where most o' the locals eat," he says.

We leave the office, and I hand the car keys through the window to Rayne. I walk to room six. Rayne moves the car closer to the room under the watchful eye of the man in the office, then carries our luggage in for us.

Audrey sinks into an armchair in the corner. "That man was a bit forward, winking at you like that, wasn't he?"

"I think he saw Rayne in the car and thought…well, you know," I say.

Rayne's face turns a bright shade of pink. "That's sick!"

"Don't worry, I told him you were my husband," I say.

Rayne shakes his head. "Oh, God! I'm starting to regret this already." He turns to leave. "You two are more like my grandmother than I first thought."

61

Audrey taps the chair beside her. "Sit down and tell us about her."

"Not right now," he says. "Maybe I will take you up on your suggestion to leave my guitar in your room though, and some of my other stuff."

From the window, I watch him open the trunk and set the guitar case gently on the ground.

"This is good," I say to Audrey. "At least if his guitar is here, we know he won't disappear. He'll have to come back to get that."

Audrey rubs her leg, the other hand fingers her cane. "He's a free spirit, eh? I wish I were young again."

"Really? I don't know if I'd want to do it all again. It's too exhausting."

"Oh, come on, that doesn't sound like you," Audrey says. "You're always the one with the plans and ideas."

"What would you do differently," I ask, "if you could start over?"

"Well, if I were young *now*, I'd have a lot more choices. Girls today can do anything, don't you think? Even become mothers when they can't have children naturally. I watched a TV show on that. They make babies in a test tube and put them in the woman's womb. If we'd been able to do that, Terry and I could have had lots of children. That was always a big thing for us. He blamed me."

"Having kids isn't all it's cracked up to be," I say. "They just end up putting you in a home and spending all your money."

"Maybe so, but we really wanted to be parents. I'm glad, in a way, that we weren't. He changed. I wouldn't want our children to see the way he yelled at me and called me names—

whore and trollop—when all I did was stop on the way home to pick up groceries or things."

"Oh, Audrey. I'm so sorry. I didn't know. You've never mentioned that before."

"I don't like to dwell on it. He's gone now and I'm here. Actually, if I were young again, I might just choose a different husband. That would solve more than one problem, wouldn't it? I might have thought more about what I wanted to do with my life, too. I might have been a queen or a race car driver or opened a restaurant, except I don't really like to cook."

"What did you do?"

"Worked in a clothing store. Sold clothes and did alterations. I always thought I'd go out on my own as a seamstress, make wedding and bridesmaid's dresses and prom gowns, but it never happened."

Rayne returns to the room. "What's up?"

"Just talking about being young again," Audrey says. "It's a main topic of discussion when you're eighty years old… or ninety-eight. I think I'm ninety-eight."

"You're not ninety-eight. The thing is, we need to get away. Every bloody day is the same. We need an adventure," I say.

"Nothin' wrong with that," Rayne agrees.

Audrey leans forward and tries to heave herself up from the deep armchair. She falls back and tries again. Rayne offers his hand and pulls smoothly until she is standing.

She steadies herself. "Anyone else hungry? Let's go to Margaret's."

"Mabel's," I say. "It's Mabel's."

We drive the short distance to the restaurant. It is

easy enough to find—lots of cars and a big front window framed by lace curtains and a neon sign in the center. As we enter, a dozen pairs of eyes look up. A young waitress comes from the back and waves to us and flashes a big smile like we're old friends.

She introduces herself to Audrey and me. Rachel. She's polite and friendly, especially to Rayne, touching his shoulder and laughing easily when he speaks. Her focus never leaves his face. When Rayne jokes with her, he has a charming smile, nice teeth and his curly, copper-colored hair gives him a young Spencer Tracy look, even if he does need a haircut and a few good restful nights of sleep.

The meal is delicious, especially the homemade Boston cream pie. I pay the bill and Audrey and I leave.

"I'll be right there," Rayne says.

Eventually he opens the car door and slides behind the wheel. There's a jauntiness to the way he holds his head.

"She's pretty," Audrey says.

"Yeah, she's okay."

Just past eight o'clock, the motel owner is behind the office window inspecting the parking lot. He watches us pull up out front and walk to the door of room six. Satisfied that it isn't a new customer, he pulls the curtain across and turns out the office light.

Audrey yawns. "I'm tired."

"Me too."

We both look at Rayne.

"If I could just wash up, I won't bother you again," he says. A few minutes later he emerges from the bathroom, clean-shaven and dressed in a fresh shirt. "G'night. I'll see you in the morning." He tosses the keys on the table.

I draw the curtains and drop down on the bed without even changing into my nightgown. My back is angry. Legs and arms melt into the mattress like butter. Audrey's breathing rumbles from the bed next to mine.

"Are you asleep?" I ask through the darkness.

No answer.

My body is heavy with exhaustion, but my mind buzzes with thoughts. I reach for my purse and pull out the pad and pen and scribble some words.

so quiet. Mabel's. darkness. Audrey. Tom?

Is Tom with us? I can't be sure. I rest on the pillow and try to silence the humming in my brain, but it won't be still. The good memories from the day are washed aside by new thoughts. *Have the nurses noticed we're gone from Tranquil Meadows? Have they phoned Carol? Has the boy noticed his car is missing? Why can't I get to sleep?*

"Oh, good Lord…our medication! We totally forgot about all our pills," I say. My arms won't cooperate when I try to push myself up, they just buckle beneath me.

"Audrey…Audrey!" I shout.

Audrey rouses to semi-consciousness. "What is it?"

"We forgot. We need our pills every day. What happens if we don't take them?"

"We'll be okay. We don't need them," Audrey mumbles.

"Yes we do. Why didn't we think of that?"

The pills are a big deal. Uniforms always ask if we took our pills: "Did you swallow your pills, Lillian?" "Here are your pills." "Where are your pills? Take this little one first.

65

It helps with the forgetting." "Take these and these."

Audrey is snoring again. The night stretches on and on. Traffic noise outside slows, and the sounds of televisions and running water from adjoining rooms become hushed. Finally, I sleep.

6

SILENCE. AND THE SMELL. Or lack of it. I have no idea where I am. Pale light filters into the room. There is someone in the bed beside mine.

She looks a bit like my sister, but I think it's Audrey. Maybe Audrey is my sister.

I open the curtains and peek outside. The fading moon is still visible; the sky's only beginning to brighten. It feels wrong to see the street from this level, though I can't place exactly why. Everything is so close and immediate, as it should be, and yet it seems odd this morning.

Cars are parked in a row along the front of the building.

A voice startles me.

"Lillian?" Audrey struggles to sit up.

"I'm sorry, did I wake you?"

"Is it morning?" She swings her legs over the side of the bed. "Where are we?"

There are things scattered around this room: a backpack, an overstuffed shopping bag, a strangely shaped case with a handle and another huge pack beside the door. What on earth is this case? I touch it. Sometimes that helps—holding things in my hand offers better clues than just looking. Nothing. I look out into the parking lot and instantly recognize a blue Intrigue, though again, I'm not sure why. A young man strolls in from the road and approaches the car. He opens the door and lies down in the back seat. Now, from where I stand, the car looks empty.

I return to the edge of the bed. "Do we have a car?"

"I believe we do," Audrey says.

"I think there's a man lying down in the back seat."

"That's Rayne, our driver." The answer seems to surprise her as much as it does me.

Rayne. I repeat the name over and over in my head. I'm in the midst of a mystery, trying to solve the case.

"We're on vacation, heading west." Audrey smiles, obviously pleased with herself. She turns on the television. A man and woman with very serious expressions pose behind a desk, but there are no words. Audrey examines the switcher-thing but can't figure out how to choose sound over silence or how to change the station, so she hands it to me. The only button that makes sense is the red one that turns it on and off. I don't want to touch the others with the arrows and signs, so I lean back on my pillow, resigned to watching it as it is.

Soon Audrey is sleeping, and I sit watching silent heads bob and turn.

As the room brightens and the stirring sounds of others

filter through the walls and into her sleep, Audrey wakes again. We move around in silence—washing, dressing, attempting to follow our morning routines. My hips snap and crack, yield slowly, mechanically.

There's a knock on the door, and a man edges into our room. "Are you ready to go?"

"Excuse me! Did someone invite you in?" I ask.

He ignores me. "I'll load up the car and we'll stop in town for breakfast before we hit the road. Mabel's okay?"

"Hit the road? What are you talking about and…who are you?" I ask. This guy has a lot of nerve!

Audrey looks at me with a blank expression, no answers hidden there.

"Are you serious?" The guy looks more closely at me. "You really don't know who I am, do you?" He stands in the doorway, staring at us for a moment, then turns and leaves the room.

My head starts to buzz. It sounds like a cicada, rising and falling, loud enough to keep me from thinking clearly. Everything is so new. I have an odd sense that this is good, and yet the muscles in the back of my neck and shoulders are tense and sore. I try to calm myself and concentrate. *This man knows us, but we don't know him.*

"Where did he go?" Audrey asks. She walks to the window, then answers her own question. "He's leaning on my car, smoking."

She leaves the room and I follow, not knowing what else to do. All around him there's the sweet scent of marijuana, like a memory siphoned from somewhere deep in the past; from the days we had a rebellious son living in the basement.

The smoke curls up from his lips. He inhales again and

waits. "What is wrong with you two?" he asks after holding his breath and, finally, exhaling. "I want the truth."

I look at the ground, still unsure of who he is or how much to trust him. "We're forgetful, that's all. We need to be reminded about things sometimes—where we are and who you are—things like that. You're going to be like us soon enough if you keep smoking that stuff, you know. It's not good for you."

"Is that right? Is that how you got this way?" he says.

"Don't be a smart ass. We're much older than you and we had better things to do with our time at your age than waste it with that silly weed. Responsible things like jobs and family. Now, tell us—who are you, and what are your intentions?"

"Rayne, I'm Rayne. We met yesterday and you asked me to drive you out west."

Unlikely but interesting. Tidbits start to flash back.

"That's my car," Audrey says. "You can drive it if you like. That's what we're using to go on our vacation."

"So, just like that it's all good now?" Rayne asks. "I'm not gonna stop smoking, so if that's an issue for you, we can say good-bye right now."

He looks at me with a challenge I recognize. It's not a fight I feel up to having just now.

"We'll see," I tell him. "Maybe I'll be smoking too, before this is over. Who knows?"

I try to ease into the idea of trusting this boy for the time being. He's cocky, but there's something familiar about him.

"I know I'm gonna fuckin' regret this," he says, "but let's try it for another day and see how it goes."

Audrey opens the car door. "Let's eat breakfast. I'm starving."

Rayne drives into town and parks in front of Mabel's. As we enter, Audrey's face lights up. "I recognize this place!"

We sit near the window. A young man approaches and pours coffee. "Good morning. I'll leave these menus and be right back to take your order."

"Excuse me," Rayne says as the boy turns to leave, "Is Rachel here this morning?"

"Nope. She doesn't work today."

"Who's Rachel?" I ask.

Rayne blushes. "We met her last night when we were here for supper. She was our waitress, remember?"

The boy returns and glares at Rayne. "I thought I recognized you when you came in. Good thing my sister wasn't scheduled for the morning shift. She was just stumbling in the door when I was leaving the house for work. But then, you know that."

Rayne takes a keen interest in the menu, avoiding eye contact with the waiter. "I'll have two eggs over easy, bacon, and toast, please—and a large milk."

"You're lucky it's me serving you and not my mom or dad. If they knew Rache was out all night with you, that hot coffee wouldn't have made it to the cup."

I wonder what they're talking about but decide to let it go.

We're comfortably settled in the Intrigue, heading west along the Trans Canada Highway. Trees and rocky terrain fly by, and I try to imagine what lies ahead. I've never been farther west than Steinbach, Manitoba. I have vivid memories of taking the train to visit a friend who had moved out there to work the summer after my first year of teaching. That was before I married Albert. My friend, Martha, was living there on her own and had fallen in with some rowdy friends who loved to party and didn't think much of working. My mom had agreed to let me go because she said that Steinbach was a "dry region"—no alcohol. She sure was wrong. My first time so far away from home with no one to answer to was full of temptation. I got drunk and flirted with boys, and I even kissed one and let him fondle my boobs, though I never told Albert. That boy asked Martha for my address and kept writing to me, asking me to come back and saying he loved me! I'll never forget the thrill of acting so irresponsibly.

In fact, I'm feeling a little like that now—naughty, unchecked. This time though, I've taken an innocent bystander along with me. Audrey is naïve. She trusts me and follows me without question.

I'm glad now that Rayne has joined us. I don't think I could have found the way. We've passed through a couple of small towns and are just entering North Bay where, according to the road signs, the Trans Canada Highway splits, one branch following Highway 17 toward Sudbury and the other turning northward along Highway 11. Rayne turns north. He seems to know by instinct which way to go. Albert is like that too. It must be something in the male chromosome. I'm pitiful where direction is concerned.

I try to visualize the place we left in Ottawa and draw a blank. I concentrate more deeply. Still nothing. My childhood home is there in full detail, the bedroom I shared with my sisters, Sharon and Susan. Are they gone now? Passed away? How can I not remember this? And the larger bedroom beside it with two sets of bunk beds for my four brothers, all gone but one—John.

I think he's still alive. He visited me recently. Yes, I'm sure of it.

My brothers always fought over the top bunks like snarly dogs fight over an old bone, just to say they won the battle.

Rayne switches on the radio, pushing button after button to find a station with something other than gardening shows for the northern temperate zone. Eventually he gives up and turns it off.

"We should sing," Audrey says. "You're a musician. Start us off on a song and we'll join in."

"Great idea," I say.

Rayne shakes his head. "No. Definitely not."

"Come on. It'll be fun," Audrey says.

"No."

"I bet you know some old songs: "You Are My Sunshine," "A Bicycle Built For Two," "Sunny Side of the Street"? Didn't you sing with your parents or your grandma in the car?"

"No. We had radios that worked and I had an MP3 player," Rayne says in a snarly tone.

Audrey starts to sing and I join in. *"You are my sunshine, my only sunshine. You make me happy when skies are gray."*

Rayne inserts his white earplugs and tries to ignore us.

"I'm getting angry," Audrey says. "Anyone else?"

"Why are you angry?" I ask.

"What do you mean? Oh jeez, not angry—I need to eat. My stomach is growling."

"Hungry?" Rayne asks. He's removed his earplugs and caught the end of the conversation.

Outside of town, several restaurants line both sides of the highway. We agree on pizza. Audrey has trouble getting out of the car. Her hips and knees are seizing up.

"I'll be fine," she says. "I may move a bit slower, but we'll call it my vacation pace." She laughs at her own joke.

The pizza is delicious. "We don't get this at Tranquil Meadows," I say, taking another bite.

Rayne eyes me with curiosity. "What's Tranquil Meadows?"

"That's the house where Audrey and I stay. They make our meals there."

"A house. You mean like a retirement lodge?" Rayne asks.

"Yeah, like that."

Back in the car, I find myself fussing with the zippers and straps on the pack beside me. I'd come close to letting our secret slip. I can't be sure Rayne will keep driving west if he knows. He might call the nursing home. The nurses will say we have to go back, I'm sure of that. We need to get farther away. I lean forward and tap him on the shoulder. "You should drive faster."

"I'm going fifteen over the limit," he says.

I envision being stopped by the police. "You should slow down."

"I'm just going with the flow of traffic," he says, his voice sounding a little edgy.

"That's good. Going with the flow is good."

Rayne glances in the mirror. "Are you sure?"

I can't believe it. I didn't see it coming, but I'm sobbing. "No, I'm not sure of anything....Damn!"

Rayne focuses on the road and drives on in silence. Audrey reaches around and pats my knee.

Outside, the scenery looks like it will swallow us up in all its untouched space. Green sprouts from rock like the crabgrass that Albert fights in the driveway cracks at home.

Houses grow fewer and farther apart, and small lakes and rivers flash silver through the trees.

"I feel like the lake is whispering to us, calling us," Audrey says. "Could we get out and walk in the woods?"

"Yes," I say, "that's why we're here. We should explore." The surroundings are relaxing me. "I'm glad I brought my running shoes. I knew they'd come in handy."

"You aren't really gonna do this, are you?" Rayne says. "We'll just stop the car and look at the woods through the open window."

"You're forgetting that your job is to drive. We make the decisions," I say. "You should come walking with us in case we need you to kill a bear or something."

"Very funny. If there's bear in there, you're on your own." Rayne pulls into a rest area at the side of the road and stops the car beside a picnic table.

"Too bad we didn't bring a picnic lunch," Audrey says.

"We already had lunch. Didn't we?"

"What did we have?"

"I made us grilled cheese sandwiches."

Rayne listens, raises his eyebrows. "We had pizza," he says. He gets out of the car and steps back. "Resourceful," he says, pointing at my shoes and smiling for the first time today. "You'll have to lead the way. My sandals won't be good for carving a path."

"I'll go first," Audrey offers, "and beat a path with my cane. It'll be useful in case we meet up with a snake."

"How deep are you planning to go?" Rayne asks. "I might wait in the car."

He reaches out to hand the keys to me.

I shake my head. "You hold on to them."

I lead the way into the trees along a wide walking path. The earth is hard and dry. The scents are heady, changing from toasty, baked dirt to the freshness of leaves and plants and fallen trees. Much of the land along the path is rocky— smooth and gray like a sculpture.

"Listen to the birds," Audrey says. She adjusts her hearing aid.

The trail narrows as we plod deeper into the woods. Out front, I tramp along in my running shoes, each step deliberate and steady. I can hear Audrey behind me, cane testing as she walks, trying to keep up. Rayne is last. Eventually, we can no longer hear the noise of traffic on the road. The snap of branches and the choir of birds are the only sounds. I'm a young mom and this is a Sunday afternoon outing with the kids.

A voice comes from behind, "That's far enough, don't you think? We should get back to the car."

I stop and look up. "Where's Carol...and Tom?" I ask. My pulse races. "Albert, where are the kids? I thought you were watching them!"

The woman behind me tries to take my hand. "It's okay, Hon. They're safe. They stayed at home."

"At home? They were with us."

"No, they're safely back at home." She holds my hand more tightly. "Walk with me back to the car. I'm getting pretty tired."

My palms grow sweaty, and I wrench my hand from hers. "Carol!" I shout. "Carol! Tom!"

The air is hot and still. "Tom," I call out as loudly as I can. "We're leaving!" My voice is raspy and weak as I try to make them hear. I walk farther into the trees, hoping to catch sight of the children. Why does this keep happening? What kind of mother am I, losing my children? My head is heavy and thick. The cicadas have returned. I slump to the ground and cry, still shouting their names between sobs.

Carol and Tom do not return. Finally, I let the people on either side guide me back out to the open space. I try to listen to what they're saying, but the words don't make sense.

The man opens the car doors. I refuse to get in.

"We can't leave them here! We have to find them."

The woman backs up to the open door and drops down onto the seat.

The man stands beside me, eyes wide. "They're not in there," he says. "We went in alone, just the three of us."

I try to wrestle past him. "Let me go. I have to find my children."

He puts a hand on each of my shoulders and won't let me past. "No, we have to leave. There are no children in there."

I glare at him, then turn and crawl into the back seat. He reaches in to help me with the seatbelt, but I push him away. He closes the door. I sit there, unable to move. By the time we pull out onto the highway I'm numb.

"What's wrong with her?" the man asks.

The woman answers something, and he nods in recognition. "Shit. I should have known." He looks over and catches her eye. "You too?"

"Yep."

"Man, that sucks."

My head is stuffed with cotton balls and clay. I listen to the voices from the front seat with my eyes closed.

The man is telling a story. "My grandma had Alzheimer's. I didn't know. She was always a little out there—you know—different, but all my life she stood up for me and encouraged me to do what I wanted. 'Follow the music' she used to say." He breathes deeply. "Before I left home, I noticed she was getting moody and forgetful, but I just thought it was normal; she was pretty old. When I told her I was moving east, she started yelling at me. 'I've looked after you all your life, and now that I need you around, you desert me! What am I supposed to do?' She freaked. I guess I was pretty self-absorbed. I should have seen the changes, but I just wanted to get the hell out of there. Anyway, she died two years ago. She was eighty. I went back for her funeral, and from the stories I heard, it sounded like she got a lot worse toward the end. It's brutal."

Is he talking about me? I open my eyes.

The woman in the front seat has fallen asleep.

The man speeds up, weaving past cars and trucks as if he's being chased. I can't take my eyes off of him. His hands grip the wheel, knuckles sharp and white. From the back seat, I can see out the windshield as he flies past exits leading to the towns and villages that have sprouted up beside the highway. I watch with a mixture of fear and excitement until he slows. His shoulders sag. He looks exhausted.

"Lillian. Audrey. Wake up," Rayne says. "It's time to stop for the night."

Audrey raises her head. "Where are we?"

"Cochrane. There are lots of motels on the highway. Do you want to be out here, or in town?"

No one answers.

I rouse myself, feeling refreshed and wondering where Cochrane is. I've heard of it, but I don't think I've ever been there.

Rayne drives on and finds a small motel near a lake in the center of town. I'm stiff and sore but glad to be arriving in a new place. The change feels right.

"I'll go in and get two rooms. You wait here." He shuts the car off and pulls the key from the ignition, then changes his mind. "I'll leave it on so the air conditioning is running," he says.

He looks at me, thoroughly checking me out, as if he thinks I might go crazy while he's gone.

"We're not going to bolt. You're the one who isn't sure about staying with us. Our minds are made up already," I say.

Rayne checks the mirror, runs his fingers through his hair, and goes inside.

Audrey reaches over and turns on the radio as she saw Rayne do earlier in the day. A news anchor's voice, serious and low, fills the car: the economic downturn, the dry spell, the latest political scandal, and then—news of two elderly residents missing from a nursing home in Ottawa, concern for their safety, and a directive urging anyone with information to contact the police.

7

AUDREY'S MOUTH DROPS open. "Did you hear that?"

"Is that us?" I ask.

"Who else? It has to be."

"People will be looking for us then?"

"We're on the news."

"On the news! We're on the news," I say. "I wonder if we're on TV—you know—with our pictures and everything. Wait. No, that wouldn't be good. Carol might see it, or Tom, and then they'd try to take us back. Did they mention the car?"

Rayne comes out of the motel office with two sets of room keys.

I poke Audrey's shoulder hard. "Turn it off, quick, and don't tell Rayne!"

He doesn't seem to even notice that we look shaken. "Okay, they asked for a credit card, but I told them you'd go in and do that as soon as you get settled. I said you are my grandma and my great-aunt."

He helps us into our room. "I'll come and get you at six o'clock."

"Okay, Dear. See you then," Audrey says.

The room is sparsely furnished with Eighties décor, dusty rose and jade green bedspreads and art that looks like splotches of paint. But it isn't like Tranquil Meadows and that's enough for me.

"I can't believe it! We're famous—on the news! What should we do?" Audrey asks.

I don't know what to say. I never dreamed our vacation would become a news story. I stare at the ugly, flowered carpet and try to think.

I'm a teacher, I can think fast on my feet. How many times have I had unexpected situations and had to make them work? Lots. "Now let me see. We can't tell Rayne yet. He might panic. And I think we should use false names, don't you, in case they release the names of the missing people?"

"Lucy and Ethel. They were good friends and they always had crazy, wild adventures. Remember *I Love Lucy*? I loved that show."

"Perfect," I say. "Can I be Lucy?"

"Sure."

"Ethel?"

"Yes, Lucy?"

"I think I'm going to just lie down here for a minute and rest my back before we go out for supper."

Audrey moves slowly around the room, opening curtains, looking through her bag, gathering all her things around her and every couple of minutes, checking on me. I lie flat on the bed, staring at the ceiling.

There's a knock at the door.

"You ready in there?" It's Rayne.

"Come on in," Audrey calls.

"I've checked around. A couple of restaurants nearby look decent. Do you feel like walking?"

Audrey taps her cane on the floor. "That's a great idea. Let's walk."

Rayne reminds me about the credit card. He rings the silver bell on the counter, and a pleasant looking, middle-aged woman appears.

"Hello again," she says to Rayne. "You must be his grand-mother and aunt. Pleased to meet you."

"Our pleasure," I say. "My grandson mentioned you wanted a credit card. Would it be all right if we simply paid cash?"

"Of course. I'll just write down your driver's license information then."

I count out the money. "I didn't bring my driver's license with me. Do you really need it?"

"Security policies require we have identification on file for people renting rooms, that's all."

Rayne pulls out his wallet and hands the lady his license. She writes down the details. "Thank you. Enjoy your visit."

Rayne leads the way down the street and around the corner. "How does this look?" he asks, pointing to a small diner, deco-rated with a ship's bell and wheel and nets hung over hefty ropes. From the front, looking farther along the street, we can see the lake with its docks and a few small boats moored alongside.

"This is good," I say.

Audrey grabs my arm and steps behind me, almost knocking me to the ground. "Whoa! What's that?" she yells.

A dog bounds up to Rayne and winds itself around his legs. It is a mid-sized, sandy-colored pup with long, shaggy hair.

Rayne bends over to pet her. "Hello, Girl." The dog leans in toward his leg and nuzzles close.

Audrey peeks out from behind me. "Jeez. I saw a ball of hair heading our way, and it scared the daylights out of me! I thought it was a wolf!"

The dog licks my hand, tail thumping a steady rhythm on the sidewalk. "You're adorable," I say.

"Be careful. It might bite you," Audrey says.

"Look at that face. She's not mean. Don't you like dogs?"

Audrey's grip loosens. "Yeah, it's just that the dogs at the farm were more like guard dogs and herding dogs. They stayed outdoors, and we didn't really pay much attention to them. They kept their distance mostly."

As we enter the diner, the dog whimpers briefly, turns full circle and curls up on the ground beside the door.

After a delicious meal, Rayne has space for a piece of carrot cake before declaring he's had enough. "I'm gonna take a walk around town."

"Oh, good, we'll go too," I say.

"I'll walk you back to the motel. I've got some places I need to go on my own," he says.

The dog is now bouncing around our feet. She follows us as we stroll back to the motel, easing into a well-behaved pace as if she knows that Audrey isn't steady on her feet and needs to be careful.

Audrey and I sit on a bench in the front garden, unable to

go any farther. The dog curls up at Rayne's feet.

"Looks like you have a new friend," Audrey says.

He scratches the dog's ears. "I wonder where she belongs. I had a dog that looked almost like this when I was younger."

"Do you still have him?" I ask.

"He got hit by a car when I was thirteen. I still remember watching it happen—hanging out, shooting baskets in the driveway. Shadow—that was his name—was watching. A motorcycle rode by. He hated the noise. He started onto the road to chase the bike, but I whistled to call him back and just as he stopped and turned, a car came around the corner and hit him."

As he's telling the story, he pets this new dog, looks her in the eyes.

"That must have been horrible."

"Yeah. Dad tried to convince me to get another one, but I couldn't do it. It didn't seem right to just replace him like a broken shoelace."

He suddenly walks away. "I gotta go. I'll probably see you in the morning." The dog stands up and watches him, her tail tucked close.

"Come on then," he says, patting the side of his leg, and they stride off, disappear around the end of the garden hedge.

"I never really liked dogs," Audrey says. "I had a cat. My dad hated cats, so I had to keep her hidden in my room or else make sure she was outside when he was home. He would get so mad if he caught her in the house. He always said if we started keeping cats in the house, then the pigs and sheep would have to come inside too."

"Didn't you know your dad hated cats when you married him?" I ask.

"When I married who? My dad?"

"Yes. You shouldn't have married him if you didn't like the same things he liked. Now take Albert and me. We're very compatible."

"I didn't marry my father," Audrey says.

"What are you talking about? Your mother married your father and then they had you. How could you have married him?" Sometimes I can't follow Audrey's thinking. She often gets confused. "It doesn't matter. What were we talking about?"

"I used to be kind of afraid of dogs, but this one seems nice. She sure likes Rayne, doesn't she? I like Rayne too. He's very sweet."

I want to argue this, to guard against this trust that Audrey has for the boy. She adores him, gushes over him. I'm not so sure.

After trying to stifle too many yawns, we go inside.

"Do you feel different since we left Tranquil Meadows?" Audrey asks.

"I'm never bored, and I like not having everything decided for us."

I stretch out on the bed. "These marshmallows are comfortable." I dream that a dog barks and barks in the night.

Rain taps steadily on the window, and I wake to the sound of a loud knock. The door rings with another, more determined knock, and a voice shouts, "Lillian, Audrey, open up! I'm getting soaked."

I toss back the covers and try to call up a sense of belonging in this room. At the door, I peer through the peephole. It's that boy, what is his name? He's huddled into the doorframe trying to stay dry. Just as I pull back and reach for the doorknob, he knocks again with such force that I almost fall backward.

I open the door a crack. "For heaven's sake, what do you want?"

"Can I come in?"

He steps inside, followed by a dripping form that immediately starts to vibrate from head to tail, releasing a smelly rain shower into the room.

"Jeez Louise!" I turn away to get out of the spray.

Audrey sleeps through the entire exchange, her hearing aid nestled in the ashtray on the bedside table.

Rayne reaches for a towel and wipes the dog's wet coat.

"Is that yours? I don't remember you having a dog."

He smiles and the dog wags her tail a couple of times, then rests her chin on the floor, eyes glued to Rayne's face.

"I wanted to talk to you and Audrey about that. I'm gonna keep her."

Audrey opens her eyes. A glazed expression clouds her face. She pulls the covers tightly around her shoulders and lies there, looking at Rayne.

He picks up her hearing aid from the ashtray and hands it to her.

"Put that down. That's mine." Audrey's hand shoots out from under the sheets and grabs it from him. The hearing aid slips from her grasp and falls to the floor, spins around, and comes to rest under the bed.

Rayne looks shocked. He moves away and stands by the window, gazing out at the gray sky.

I kneel carefully and sweep my arm under the bed.

"Don't be like that," I say, handing the hearing aid to Audrey, "This boy's our friend. Do you remember him?"

Audrey looks more closely at him and shakes her head. She closes her eyes and feigns sleep.

"Maybe I should wait in my room," Rayne says. He and the dog leave, closing the door without a sound.

I sit on Audrey's bed and hold her hand until she's fully awake. "Mornings aren't our best time, eh Ethel?"

"Yeah, I guess you're right. Did that man have a dog?"

"I think he does now," I say.

"Is he your son?"

"No." I say. "He's the young man who's driving us around on our cruise. You were the one who convinced me to let him join us."

"We're going on a cruise?"

"I didn't say cruise. I said holiday—driving us on our holiday."

"And the dog?"

I laugh. "I guess the dog will be traveling with us too. Our family is growing, Ethel."

Audrey is quick to answer. "She's not sitting with me in the front seat."

We drag our bags to the door. Rayne is sitting in the car, his dog beside him in the passenger seat, both looking out the windshield between the back and forth of the wipers.

Rayne spreads out a blanket he finds in the trunk on one side of the back seat and gestures to the dog to get back there. He wipes down the front seat and steps away so Audrey can get in.

"I have someone to sit with now," I say, sliding in beside her. "Does she have a name?"

"I've been calling her Shadow—out of habit, I guess," Rayne says.

"I think Shadow's a great name since she follows you around like one."

He nods and turns to Audrey. "She's really well behaved."

"Don't worry about it. I like dogs now," she says. "Can we get some breakfast?"

We stop at a store to buy dog food, a large jug of water, a couple of plastic bowls, and a collar and leash, then park under a big tamarack outside a homey little café on the edge of town.

"Where are you taking us?" Audrey asks. She limps to the door and turns around to see Shadow looking out through the windshield. "There's someone trying to steal the car," she hollers, pointing and waving her cane in the air.

"It's just the dog." I try to calm her. "It's Shadow."

"He's taking the car," she insists.

"No she's not. She's just waiting in there for us while we have our breakfast."

Audrey turns to Rayne. "You didn't leave the keys in there, did you?"

"No." He takes them from his pocket and shows her. He looks unnerved.

I lace my arm through his and walk to the door. "She'll be fine. Just act normal."

Audrey follows us to a table by the window. A waitress pours three cups of coffee.

"I don't want coffee. I want tea," Audrey says.

"Oh, I'm sorry, Ma'am. I'll get you a pot of tea." The girl takes the cup away and returns, smiling brightly. "Have you decided what you would like to eat? Our special is very good."

Audrey speaks up. "I would hope your special would be good. It should be special, don't you think?"

"Yes, I suppose it should." She glances at Rayne with a look that begs for a friendly response.

"Sorry. Yes, I'd like the special please." He flashes a warm smile.

"Me too," I add.

"I'll take the special too," Audrey says. "And where's *my* coffee?"

The waitress stammers. "I…I'm sorry. I thought you said you didn't want coffee. I'm making tea for you."

Audrey shoos her away with a wave of her hand. "Fine, fine. Just bring me something hot."

When the waitress is out of hearing range, I lean in toward Audrey. "Dear, are you not feeling well this morning?"

"What do you mean?"

"Well, you're acting a little unreasonable—so unlike you."

"I guess I'm feeling distance…dissolved…distorted. Ohhh! What is the word?"

"Disoriented?" Rayne offers.

"Yes. My head feels cloudy and I feel sad and kind of angry."

The waitress returns with a pot of tea and sets it down, then darts away before Audrey changes her mind again.

"I think you've scared that poor girl silly," I say. "On the upside, we should get excellent service."

The waitress returns right away with three plates brimming with food. Just as quickly, she leaves and reappears with ketchup and a fresh pot of coffee for refills.

Audrey catches her eye. "Listen, Dear. I'm sorry for being rude. I know it isn't a good excuse, but I'm having a bad day."

The waitress fixes her gaze on Audrey's face, then on mine. She pours the coffee slowly, deliberately, as if trying to give herself enough time to figure out how to phrase her words just right. Then—"Are you from Ottawa?" she asks.

No one says a word. The waitress focuses on me. "Are you those two ladies that escaped from the nursing home in Ottawa a few days ago?"

Rayne's eyes grow wide.

I'm the first to speak. "Of course not. I know the ones you mean. I heard it on the radio. Terrible. I hope they're okay. Did you hear their names?"

The waitress looks unconvinced. "I did, but I don't remember what they were—typical old-lady names."

I hold Rayne's gaze as I speak, my eyes pleading for him to stay quiet. "I'm Lucy and this is my friend, Ethel. And this is Rayne," I add.

He sits silently, allowing the facts to sink in.

The waitress laughs. "Lucy and Ethel? Like on that old TV show?" She turns to Rayne. "Is she telling the truth?"

He forces a weak smile and nods. "Lucy and Ethel. That's them. Crazy, eh? You sure you don't remember the names of the two that ran away from the nursing home?"

"No, but I know it wasn't Lucy and Ethel. I would have remembered that. I heard it on the news last night. Two older ladies with Alzheimer's have gone missing from a nursing home in Ottawa and their families and friends are really worried. The police are asking people to be on the lookout for them in Ottawa."

Sweat trickles down Rayne's forehead. He wipes it with his napkin and excuses himself to use the washroom.

The waitress stares at us. Audrey picks up her fork and digs into her eggs and sausage. "I hope they find those poor women," she says, between bites. "It'll be a real shame if anything happens to them."

"Yeah. Is that guy okay? He didn't look very good," the waitress says.

"My grandson? He's fine, thank you. He's just been working too hard lately." I assure her that we are simply heading home after visiting relatives in Mattawa and dismiss her with polite thanks for her concern.

Rayne returns and takes a seat at the table. He refuses to look at Audrey and me, just shovels food into his mouth, forcing himself to swallow. He finishes his coffee in one gulp and then leaves the restaurant. When we join him outside, he is standing in the shelter of the doorway out of the rain. Without a word we take our places in the car.

"Good breakfast, eh?" I say. "We should get going though. We could cover a lot of distance today in this rain."

Shadow bounces from the back seat to the front and licks Rayne's hand, her rear end leaning on Audrey's lap, then jumps back again to lie on her blanket beside me. Rayne doesn't make a move to start the car. He just sits there looking back and forth at us.

He finally speaks, his voice edgy and sharp. "You *escaped* from a nursing home? And don't try to scam me. I need to know the truth."

"Escaped is not really the word I would use," I say. "It seems wrong when you say it like that. We left The Home to go on a little holiday, that's all."

"You left without telling anyone?"

"They wouldn't have let us go if we'd told them. They don't trust us," I say. "We have to be walked by someone else, just like a dog, even to go on the elevator. They never would have let us go."

Rayne stares out through the windshield. "What's so horrible about where you live? Do they abuse you? I'm trying to understand why you're so adamant about running away."

I try to remember why we left. "It's like we're already dead. Outside everyone forgets about us. Inside people talk about us when we're standing right there; make decisions for us without asking. We're invisible. I don't even want to get up in the mornings. There's more, too. I just don't feel like telling you right now."

Audrey listens, hands folded in her lap, thumbs circling round and round each other in a soothing rhythm. "You'll stay with us, won't you? We're family now."

Rayne's face softens for a second, then he focuses his attention back out the window. "And the car?"

"It was Audrey's car until she sold it to a neighborhood boy. Tell him, Audrey." I continue. "We borrowed it for our trip. How else would we get around?"

"Does he know?"

"Who?"

"The owner of the car. Does he know you have it?"

"Not exactly." I try to smile, but it feels more like a grimace. "No, he doesn't, but there's no need to speak to us in that tone of voice. We haven't done anything wrong."

Rayne grabs the steering wheel with both hands and leans his forehead against it. "So, I'm transporting runaways across the country in a stolen car." He sits up straight and slams his fist on the dash. "Shit! Damn it, Lillian! Do you have any idea how much trouble I'm in with this? The cops are gonna catch up with you, and who are they gonna blame? Two old ladies with money and serious dementia issues? Or a homeless guy with nothing in his pockets and a record showing a couple of petty charges and vagrancy? I'm such an idiot."

He closes his eyes and for a moment, the only movement is in the muscles of his jaw as he grinds his teeth forward and back. "I should have followed my gut. I wondered who the hell would let two people with Alzheimer's go on a trip by themselves, but I figured they must know better than me. Jesus, Lillian. What were you thinking?"

I sit back in my seat. "What kind of petty charges?"

Rayne looks annoyed.

"Never mind," I say. "Don't worry. You're innocent and so are we."

"Yeah? And you're crazy!" He swears again and pounds on the steering wheel. The car is suddenly cavernous. Shadow's panting fills the spaces between us.

Audrey stares at Rayne as if trying to figure out who has suddenly taken his place. She shakes her finger at him, the skin on the back of her upper arm swaying and rippling. "You stop your swearing. There's no need for that," she says, then, matter-of-factly, "We're not crazy. Having Alzheimer's doesn't mean you're crazy."

"Stealing a car and running away from everything—that's crazy whether you have Alzheimer's or not."

"You ran away from everything," I say.

"Two really big differences: I told my dad I was leaving and I didn't steal someone's car. I get the leaving part, but the rest is just bad planning. You had to know you were gonna cause trouble doing it that way."

"No," I say, "we just decided, and we did it. We aren't hurting anyone."

Rayne struggles to fit the key in the ignition. His hands are shaking. "You need to go to the police and let them know where you are and tell them your story about the car."

We both answer together. "No!"

"Oh yeah, you have to. People are worried about you, not to mention if we get stopped, I'm goin' down as the bad guy. You can count on that."

"No, we can't go to the police. We haven't done anything wrong, and I'm not ready to go back yet."

Rayne shakes his head. "Except for the car! That's a huge exception. That's a major theft charge, and I can't risk that falling on me. I have to go. You two are on your own." His voice grows softer as he comes to this conclusion.

Audrey looks terrified.

A chill sweeps across the back of my neck and down my arms "Do you really think anyone would think badly of you for helping out two old ladies with Alzheimer's?" I ask. I take hold of his sleeve. "I'd be proud of my son if he did something so kind. We'll be lost without you. Can't you stay?"

"There's no way we're gonna make it all the way to B.C. without getting caught in this stolen car," Rayne says.

"How will they know it's stolen?" I ask. My thoughts start to jangle more loosely. I feel a lump rising in my throat and my voice is shaky. "Maybe the boy next door didn't even report it missing. Maybe he's away on vacation too."

Audrey perks up. "Oh! What month is this? His family

always goes away in the summer. I bet they're not even home. They don't even know!"

Rayne looks doubtful. "How old is this kid? He's old enough to drive. He wouldn't go with his parents to their cottage. He'd have a summer job, a girlfriend. He wouldn't go."

"Maybe not," I say, "but we don't know that."

"Yeah," Audrey adds.

"Is that part of the disease? You believe whatever far-fetched fantasy suits your purpose?" Rayne says.

Water streams down the windows. Shadow lays her chin on my lap and whimpers softly until I stroke her head again and again.

"You need to go back," Rayne says.

Audrey turns to face me. "Maybe he's right."

"No. I'm not going back yet." I refuse to look at her.

Rayne takes the keys from the ignition, pops the trunk, and hands the keys to me. "You'll have to go on alone then. I can't risk being involved." We listen as he shifts things around in the trunk and removes his guitar and large pack. He opens the door and calls Shadow to follow him. She stands on the seat, tail drawn close to her back legs. She turns and licks me before jumping out beside Rayne.

"Best of luck," he says. "I hope you make it to the Rockies. They're unbelievably beautiful; worth seeing at least once." He closes the door and walks away with Shadow close behind, rain drizzling down, soaking everything.

8

WE WATCH THEM GO, sitting in the car long after they're out of sight. Finally, I move from the back seat into the front behind the steering wheel and fit the key into the ignition. "Are you with me?"

"I'm with you," Audrey says. "Let's see the Rockies."

I accelerate slowly toward the road, look left and right, then left again, then back at Audrey. "Which way do we go?"

Audrey looks up and down the road through the rain. She points to the left. I pull out and crest the small hill. Rayne and Shadow are walking along the shoulder of the road.

"Stop and pick them up, they're getting drenched," Audrey says.

I pull over just past them and wait for them to approach.

Audrey rolls down the window and shouts, "Come on, hop in. We'll give you a lift."

Rayne keeps walking without acknowledging us.

"Yoohoo. Hello," Audrey shouts, "Come and get dry."

"Get away from me," he says as he passes the car. "I don't know you."

"It's Audrey and Lillian. You know us," Audrey says. She turns and looks at me, her brow wrinkled. "He says he doesn't know us."

I pull back out onto the pavement. "We don't need him."

Audrey watches out the rear window until they are out of sight. The traffic is light and I set my own pace—slow and steady. Trucks and cars come from behind, gain on us, and pass like we're standing still, sometimes with an impatient honk of their horns, nearly sending us over the edge of the road.

I try to watch for signs and point them out to Audrey as we pass. "We're near a place called Moonbeam," I say. "Why don't you see if you can find that on the map?"

She's still looking for that when I notice a sign for the city of Kapuskasing. Just off the highway, there is a huge grocery store. "Let's buy some fruit and cookies and things to make sandwiches. We'll have a picnic later," I say.

Driving in the parking lot is a little like driving in downtown Ottawa—one-way streets, stop signs everywhere, and cars zipping in and out of spaces without warning till you nearly want to scream. We park quite a distance from the store because there is more room to maneuver, and with the rain pouring down, it is very hard to see clearly. We head for an expanse of wall, hoping to find a door, not visible from where we are.

"It's got to be behind that wall."

"What does?" Audrey asks.

"The door. We need to get inside, or how else will we buy what we need?"

"No need to get snarky," Audrey says. "Just having a hard time keeping up with the plans. You could be more clear, you know."

We follow some other people to a door that's hidden behind a jutting wall. The store is cold and bright and there are rows and rows as far as we can see, and farther. In the vegetable and fruit section, waxy produce shines in mountains of color. We round a corner and find ourselves surrounded by bins of candies and nuts and spices. Spying a bin of Jujubes, Audrey reaches in and takes a handful. She pops a couple in her mouth and offers some to me.

There are so many aisles filled with baking supplies, cleaning products, cereal, crackers, soup, bags and bags of chips, and every kind of pop you can imagine.

"Can we get chips?" Audrey asks.

"Sure."

Up and down the aisles we go until we've made our way through the whole store.

"My back is killing me," I say. "Let's go."

We find the door and start through.

"Excuse me, Ma'am."

I turn to see who is speaking.

"Did you pay for those chips?"

I look at Audrey, surprised to see the bright blue bags of chips in her hand. "Oh, for heaven's sake, I'm sorry. What do we need to do?" I fumble in my purse, embarrassed at having to be reminded. "How much are they, Dear?"

The clerk places her hands on her hips. "Oh, no. You don't

fool me. You people are the worst—pretending you've forgotten. *Please!* You need to speak with the manager." She plucks the bags from Audrey's arms and picks up a microphone. "Grocery Manager to cash, please. Grocery Manager to cash."

The announcement blares through the whole store and before long, a very large, baby-faced young man eases up beside the cashier.

The woman points at Audrey and me and waves the bags of chips in the man's face. "They tried to walk out with these," she says, as if "these" are diamonds or pearls.

I can feel Audrey moving closer until she is leaning on me, her hand shaking and her breathing heavy.

The man wipes sweat from his forehead, even while I shiver from the cold. "I have to ask you to come with me, ladies," he says, looking at us for the first time.

"The hell we will," I say in a very loud voice. "Forget the chips. Are you saying we tried to steal them? We'll never shop here again, and we'll tell all our friends to stay away from… what's the name of this store, anyway?"

The man tries to hush me with a wave of his hand. "No need to get upset, Ma'am. Just follow me."

He shuffles around the end of the conveyer belt, motioning for us to follow. Audrey looks at me for direction.

"We will do no such thing," I say. "What do we know about you and what you have in mind for us? Two respectable women traveling alone have to be careful. Whatever you have to say to us, you can say it right here in front of all these people, young man."

"Look," he says, blushing several shades of red. "I'm a manager here, and I can't just let customers walk out of the store with food they haven't paid for. Now, you did not pay for those chips, am I right?"

"We forgot. We would have noticed and come back to pay. Good grief, we're not thieves. We're hungry and—did I mention—I have excruciating pain thundering up and down my spine, and the longer we stand here, the worse it gets?"

His face puffs up until I think it will explode, and he flashes a disapproving look at the cashier. "All right. Look, we'll just let it go this time. If you want the chips, you just need to pay for them and we'll be happy to send you on your way."

The cashier stares him down and mumbles something under her breath. He stays and watches as she swipes the chips across the scanner and tucks them into a grocery bag. She takes the money I offer and hands me the change. "There you go," she says. "Have a nice day."

Outside, the sun has broken through the clouds. Audrey grabs my arm and laughs. "That was like a rollercoaster ride. First you want it to be over and when it is, you want to do it again."

Exhaustion grips my back and pinches it into spasms of pain. "I can't go any farther. I have to sit down."

"There's nowhere to sit. Come on, you can do this, just a little farther," Audrey urges.

My eyes start to water. "I don't know where the car is."

"We'll find it, don't cry. Look, there are a couple of young men who will help us." She waves her arms and calls to them as if they're old friends. "Hello. Excuse me. Could you help us find our car?"

"Oh, God. Has it come to this?" I say.

The two hoodlums jostle each other and scuff their way over to us. "Watsup?"

One of the boys pushes his friend forward. "You lost?"

The other boy looks at me and then scans the lot.

Audrey reaches her hand out to greet the boy who spoke. With one swift motion, he grabs her purse and pushes her down. The two of them run through the lot, disappearing into the maze of trucks and vans. Audrey sits motionless and stunned on the pavement.

"Are you all right?" I ask, bending over her. "Those, those—cowardly little bullies! Can you move your legs?"

A young mother, holding her toddler, rushes over to help. "I'll call an ambulance and the police," she says, looking for her cell phone.

"No. No, don't do that just yet," I say. "Audrey, can you move?"

Audrey swivels a little so she is sitting straight and lifts her knees. "I went down in slow motion," she says. "It was the strangest feeling."

"I'm calling the police. Those boys can't get away with that," the woman says. She's dialing 911.

"No, please don't," I say. "We're in a hurry, and we don't want to make a fuss." I take Audrey's hand and the woman helps to hoist her up from behind.

"This is crazy. We need to report this," the woman insists. She hands Audrey the cane lying on the ground. "Those kids took your purse."

"I'm all right." Audrey takes one step and then another. "Look. I can walk. Now, if we can just find our car, I can rest. I'll be fine."

"There you go, see? You're disoriented. You don't even know where your car is. You should get checked out in the emergency room." The woman chases after her toddler who has slipped away from her grasp. "Let me at least help you find your car."

"It's an Oldsmobile Intrigue, blue," Audrey says, as if rhyming off her own name.

"I remember that we parked away from the other cars so it would be easier," I say, pointing toward the back of the lot. We find the car with the lady's help, and although Audrey struggles to walk the distance, she insists the woman not call the police. The little boy starts fussing and crying, kicking to break away from his mom. The woman hesitates, then gives in and wishes us well. Before we drive away, I see her dialing someone on her phone.

My head is spinning, fogging up so that I have to pull over in the lot and turn off the car. I can't drive. I need time to sort out all that has happened.

"If Rayne was here, he would have fixed those boys but good," Audrey says. "Who were they anyway? Did you know them?"

"No. They were hooligans, criminals in the making. You can't be asking for help from just anyone like that. We need to discuss it first and decide who's safe. You're too trusting."

"I'm sorry."

"No, stop apologizing. I'm sorry."

We stare out the window, too tired to think about what to do next. "Did they take the chips?" Audrey asks.

The bag is lying beside my purse in the back seat. "I must have held onto it without realizing it," I say. We eat one whole bag, savoring the salt and crunch. We watch the steam rising from the pavement.

"You must be sore," I say when we finish eating. "Should we find a hospital?"

"No, I'll be fine. I'd better get home though. Terry's going to wonder where I am. He doesn't like it when I stay out too long. Can you take me home?"

"What do you mean? Does he get mad?"

"Sometimes." Audrey looks away. "Sometimes he yells at me and calls me names, or he just doesn't talk to me for days. Other times it's worse."

"He's a bully too," I say. "He's no better than those boys who pushed you down."

"He's not a…he's not that. He loves me," she says. "Please take me home now."

"We're not going home. We're going back onto the highway and we're getting away from this place and all the places we live. Come on. Get out your map and tell me which way to turn."

"You don't always get to decide," Audrey says. "I want to go home."

"Nope. Sorry. You signed up, and now you're stuck with me. Lucy and Ethel are on the move."

It feels like we've been traveling for days. I have no idea how far we've come since leaving Rayne, but birthdays and anniversaries and graduations have surely passed. We find the access to Highway 11 and slowly, carefully merge with the traffic. Why are they honking at me? I speed up when I feel more comfortable, but mostly I stay in the right lane, in case I need to pull over for some reason. I like to be prepared.

Audrey is afraid to watch the cars speed by so she looks only to the right.

"Stop!" she yells. "Pull over." She grabs my arm.

I slam on the brakes and swerve to the right. Two figures on the shoulder of the road jump off into the grass.

"My God, what was that?" I say, every nerve in my body alive and prickling. I maneuver the car to a halt and let go of the wheel. "What was that all about?"

"It was Rayne and the dog," she says.

"That's impossible. You nearly made me kill someone back there. Don't ever do that again."

Audrey opens the door and hollers back to the figures on the side of the road. "Hey, Rayne. It's us: Audrey and Lillian."

In the rearview mirror, I see them approaching. She's right. It is Rayne, and he looks furious. I think about driving away, but physically I just can't. I am shaking so badly I can barely breathe.

"What the hell do you think you're doing? Are you trying to kill me?" he says as he stands by the door. "How did you even make it this far driving like that?" He drops his bag and case on the ground and kneels down to check on Shadow. "You okay, girl?"

"We made it here just fine, thank you very much," I say. "Is she all right?"

He nods. "She's fine, but how many others did you run over between here and Cochrane?"

"You are so bitter. Did you ever think you'd be much happier if you weren't so judgmental?" I ask. "How did you get here?"

"Got a ride with a guy in a truck. He was only going as far as Kapuskasing."

Audrey tries to shift around in her seat to see Rayne better but lets out a squeal. "Oooh, that hurts," she says. "Some kid pushed me down in the parking lot."

"What?" Rayne asks.

"Yeah, pushed me right down and stole my purse," Audrey says. "You should have been there."

"What are you talking about?" he moves closer to the door.

"We bought chips and then two boys stole my purse and ran away."

"No way. You're making this up, trying to trick me into getting back in the car."

Audrey starts to pull at the waistband of her pants. "Do you want to see the bruises?"

"No. I do not." Both he and the dog are still damp and smell of wet canvas and dog hair. Except for the whiskers, Rayne looks like a little boy, lost on the highway with his dog.

"Hop in," I say. "We can at least take you to the next town and get something to eat."

"Only if I'm driving," he says.

The door opens and the back seat fills with sloppy, wet dog. I hand Rayne the keys and move to the back seat. The smell of marijuana lingers on him. He moves away and loads everything into the trunk.

"Welcome aboard," Audrey says, clapping her hands and smiling. "He's back, Lillian."

"I didn't take the dog food," Rayne says.

"You got back in the car because you didn't take the food for Shadow?" Audrey asks.

"Partly, and partly because my guitar was getting destroyed in the rain."

I laugh. "You are so full of shit!"

Rayne actually smiles. "Okay, maybe you're right. I couldn't stop thinking that my grandma would kick my ass if she knew I'd abandoned you, too."

"Woohoo! Thank you, Grandma," I say.

He pours some dog food into a bowl and places it on the floor of the back seat. He pulls back out onto the highway. The sun is shining now and the rock that stretches straight up on both sides of the road glitters like broken crystal. Each time there is a place where a level bit of rock juts out, there are figures made of stones piled on top of each other, balancing there like dancers.

"I always wonder who stops the car and climbs out on the rock face to build those things," Rayne says. "I read that officials have to go around dismantling the ones constructed by hikers because people confuse them with the landmark inukshuks that are there to mark the trails."

Audrey looks at him in awe. "Is that true? I've never even heard the word *inukshuk* until now, let alone seen one. You're very intelligent."

"Right. I've already said I'm coming along for now. No need to flatter me."

What are they talking about? *Nut ships?* I haven't noticed any ships along the road.

"Did you buy food while I was gone?" Rayne asks.

There is just one bag of chips on the seat beside me. "Could you stop and get something in the next town?" I ask.

We wait in the car while Rayne makes a quick stop and returns with two grocery bags filled with food. Back on the road, he dips one hand into the plastic bag beside him, his other hand gripping the steering wheel. He pulls out three small paper bags and hands one to each of us. Inside, there is a sandwich, neatly wrapped in clear plastic, two cookies, and an apple. "Lunch from the deli," he says, "and for dessert we have chips."

Signs point to villages and towns hidden down isolated roads. Shadow sits beside me, drooling and swallowing whole the scraps of meat and cookie I share with her.

"We should have a dog at home," I say, "for company. It would do those old folks good to have something else to think about besides themselves, don't you think, Fraise?"

She nods. "And the kids there too, sitting around watching TV all day. They should be out playing and walking a dog."

"Who's Fraise?" Rayne asks.

I lean forward for emphasis. "Fraise—you know—my aunt. She's sitting right beside you."

He drives on without comment.

"Tom, how can you pretend not to know Fraise? She's your great-aunt. You've met her many times, and Dess too. I'm very close to my mother's sisters. They're really more like my sisters than aunts. Why are you acting like you don't know her?"

Fraise doesn't seem to mind. "These sandwiches are great. Can I have some chips please?"

"They try to poison us with the food at The Home. It has a funny taste," I say. "Actually, it doesn't have any flavor at all, but that's the thing about poison. It can do that. It can taste invisible."

I tap Fraise on the shoulder. "Do you remember the dish you used to make that was like shepherd's pie with hamburger and vegetables and potatoes, and then you'd crunch chips on top? That was great. Maybe you could make that again when we get back home."

"I don't remember," she says. "Terry wouldn't like that. He hates shepherd's pie."

Rayne tries the radio and finds a station that plays music.

"I have to go pee," Audrey says as we pass a picnic rest stop area.

"Why didn't you say so when you saw the signs that said rest stop ahead?" Rayne asks.

"I didn't see them."

"Can you wait? There'll probably be another stop in a half hour or so."

"No, I have to go now," Audrey says.

"Me too," I say.

Rayne slows and pulls to a stop on the side of the highway. "I'm gonna have to wait until there's nothing coming behind us and back up," he explains.

"Just let us out here. We'll go in the long grass," I say.

"No. You're not doing that. Stay in the car."

"I've done it plenty of times, don't worry about me."

"Do not open the door," Rayne orders. "I'm putting it in reverse." He swings his right arm over the back of the seat and turns to look out the rear window; drives slowly along the shoulder of the road.

Very impressive. "Good job."

"Nice driving."

"Be careful."

Before going into the concrete building that holds the washrooms, Audrey opens the trunk of the car. She rifles through her shopping bag and pulls out two of the adult-sized diapers, tucks them under her arm and makes her way to the washroom.

Inside her cubicle, Audrey shoves one of the diapers to me under the divider. "This will solve our problem of having to stop when it's not convenient," she says.

"You're a genius," I say. "Where did you get these?"

We emerge from the building. "We're ready if you are," Audrey calls to Rayne, who joins us and corrals Shadow into the back seat.

"We shouldn't need to stop again for awhile," Audrey says, a proud look spreading across her face.

"Please don't explain," Rayne interrupts. "I don't need to know everything."

9

GERALDTON. BEARDMORE. The signs whiz by.

"My hip is really aching," Audrey says. "Can we stop here?"

"We're gonna drive a bit longer if we can, maybe to Nipigon or even Thunder Bay," Rayne says. "The farther we go, the better chance we have of making it out of Ontario without getting caught."

"Can we get out and stretch our legs?"

"Soon."

Stands of evergreens blur as we pass along the highway. Rayne slows and turns onto a secondary road cut through black-green rock that soars taller than a four-story building. "This leads into a national park," he says. "We'll just go down here and get out for a stretch. I'm sure Shadow could use a run."

We pull over by a small lake. A blue heron in the shallows watches our arrival until Shadow jumps from the car. The bird takes flight in slow motion; four steps on spindly legs, then the spread of long, bony wings. It's like watching a giraffe try to fly.

At the water's edge, Audrey's cane sinks deep into the black sand, making it hard for her to balance. I hold her hand.

Shadow darts back and forth like the silver ball inside the pinball machines my brothers used to play at the arcade. She sniffs the air and the ground and runs into the lake, lapping up water. Rayne picks up a stick and periodically tosses it ahead. A cool breeze off the lake whiffs over our skin and up the hill on the opposite side of the road. The rocky cliff, covered with trees, slopes gradually toward the peak.

Rayne draws the stick back behind his head. Shadow follows the movement, concentrating deeply, waits until it is airborne, then turns and takes off. Sand sprays up from her hind feet as she dashes forward. She reaches the stick just as it lands, but she doesn't pick it up. A sudden movement catches her attention. A giant rabbit leaps up and hurtles forward through the trees, back and forth, left and right. Shadow takes up the chase and disappears into the woods.

Rayne runs after her. "Shadow. Shadow! Shadow, come here." He crosses the road and into the trees, following Shadow's path until he too, disappears.

We watch for a long time, then find a smooth, worn driftwood log halfway up the beach and lean against it.

"What should we do?" Audrey asks.

"Wait. What else is there to do? We need to wait."

Audrey leans her cane against the wood and wiggles around until she's as comfortable as possible on this hard chunk of dried wood. "We're having fun, aren't we? I'm glad we came." She smiles and grips my hand again in hers.

I squeeze gently. "It sure beats playing bingo, doesn't it?"

Over the water the sun is low, turning the sky ballerina shades of pink and purple. "'Red sky at night, sailors' delight,' my dad used to say."

"Red sky in the morning, sailors take warning." Audrey finishes the rhyme.

"I have one," I say. "Dog chases rabbit, terrible habit."

Audrey adds her own. "Rayne chases dog, we sit on a log."

Water slaps quietly onto the shore. After what seems like an eternity, Rayne emerges from the woods farther down the road. He strolls toward us, scanning the trees. As he gets closer, I see his worried expression.

"She didn't come back while I was gone?" he asks.

"No, we haven't seen her."

"I can't believe she ran off like that. I couldn't see any sign of her in there." He paces back and forth, keeping his eyes on the tree line. "Those woods are thick, and I've called her until my throat's raw. I went in as far as I could. There's no path. We'll have to wait here and hope she comes back before dark." He calls Shadow's name again.

The daylight changes to a softer shade of blue-gray. The breeze that cooled us earlier has died away, leaving stillness except for the buzz of mosquitoes.

"Rayne," I say, "These bugs are driving me crazy. Can we go?"

He looks helpless, like a small boy who has to choose between one friend and another. "I can't leave. What if Shadow comes back and we're not here?"

"Oh yeah. I'm sorry," I say. "Do we have any food?"

He moves the car off the side of the road onto the beach

to a spot where a stand of trees and long grass hides it from passersby. He returns with a blanket and apples and cookies and chips that we didn't finish at lunch and lays the blanket in front of the log. We eat the leftovers and watch the sun disappear. In the dark there are no mosquitoes.

"This is kind of fun," Audrey says. "Do you want to stay here all night and wait for Shadow?"

"Yeah. We'll camp out under the stars," I say. "I think I'm here for good now anyway. I'll never get up off the ground without a crane to help me up."

Rayne still looks worried. "I'll take you into the nearest town and find a hotel and then come back out here myself."

"No, I want to stay."

"Me too," Audrey says. She leans over and whispers, "I'm glad we have the Depends."

Rayne stands. "I'm gonna check the glove compartment for a flashlight and have one more quick look for Shadow."

We watch the beam of light move across the road and into the trees. It bounces off trunks and leaves, accompanied by the voice shouting for Shadow in the blackness. The beam eventually changes direction and returns to the beach, focused in an ellipse on the sand. Darkness surrounds us except for that patch of light and the reflection of the moon off the water.

"She's gone," Rayne says. His face in the pale glow looks as if it will dissolve like melting snow.

"Let's start a fire," I say, desperate to make it better. "Maybe she'll see it and come back."

Rayne slumps down and lights a cigarette. The scent drifts up around us.

"Can I have some of that?" I ask.

"Not a good idea," he says, inhaling deeply and holding his breath.

"I know it's pot. I want to try it."

"You ever smoked a joint?" he asks.

"No, but I used to smoke Export Plain when I was younger. No filter. It can't be much worse than that."

He hands it to me. I inhale. There is a horrible scorching in my throat, like sandpaper on fire. I cough violently, smoke wafts into my nose and blasts out of my mouth. When I look up with tears streaming down my cheeks, Rayne and Audrey are staring at me.

Embarrassed, I take another drag, hoping this time it will be better. It burns just as much, but I manage to inhale some of the smoke into my lungs. I can barely see through the tears as I pass the joint to Audrey.

She pushes it away.

Rayne takes a few more puffs and offers it back to me. When it is gone, I turn my head a little too quickly, and it's like someone has spun me around by the arms like we used to do when we were children. I'm dizzy and giddy.

I try to get up but can't. It's not because of the pain in my back. That's gone. It's because my legs and arms are boiled spaghetti, all wobbly and loose.

"Oops, I nearly fell over." I push myself back up to a sitting position. "Wow, it's like that in-between place when I'm just about asleep, like I'm floating."

Rayne looks around. "I like your idea of having a fire."

"We'd better not," Audrey says. "Not now. You two are loopy."

Rayne piles some rocks and stones in a large ring, digs

some into the sand and stacks others on top. Maybe he's building a house. I hope we don't have to go inside. He gathers undergrowth and dead wood from the edge of the forest, pulls it inside the little wall, and lights it. He pushes the driftwood log nearer the fire, away from the smoke. How he can do all that physical work when I can barely move my arms is amazing to me.

I can't stop smiling. "This is a grand adventure!"

"You said it." Audrey drops down onto the log. "I can die happy now."

Rayne is suddenly serious. "Don't say that, don't ever say things like that."

"You're superstitious!" I say, "It's funny; I'm not afraid of dying anymore. I don't know when that changed for me."

"You're getting closer to the day you'll—" He stops. "You've seen your friends die, and your husband. I guess you've had to come to terms with it."

"I can't say I've thought it through in that much detail. I'm not planning to fly the coop any time soon, I'm just not afraid to know it will happen."

Audrey is quiet, her eyes riveted on the flame and her body swaying slightly from side to side.

"Audrey, are you okay?"

I put my arm around her shoulders and we stare at the fire.

"I need to sleep. I'm dead-tired," she says.

Rayne walks with her to the car and clears the back seat so she can lie on it. He places her cane on the floor, sets her glasses carefully in the back window and helps her slide comfortably inside, legs drawn up and head resting on his rolled-up hoodie. He closes the door softly.

I watch, marveling at his gentle manner. "Why are you here?" I ask on our way back to the fire.

"Do you mean why did I decide to get back in the car and keep going, or why am I here, existentially speaking?" He flashes a teasing grin. "Honest answer? I don't know. It goes against all logic, but I have to stay and see this through."

I put my arm through his. "Thank you."

Rayne spreads his sleeping bag out beside the log and offers it to me to use as my bed for the night. I gladly accept and fall quickly to sleep, rising and falling from consciousness with the soft strumming of a guitar and Rayne's voice floating in barely audible melodies a few feet away.

A nurse opens the curtains surrounding my bed and shakes me roughly by the shoulders. My arms just squirm around and her hands make mushy dents in my muscles. I feel it but I can't respond. I try to tell her to stop, to leave me alone but no words come. She goes away and then Carol comes and says she is moving to Africa—no—Argentina, and that she won't ever come back. She says she has work to do there, that it's very important and then she laughs and walks out. Others come too but their faces blur and disappear. My head feels like someone is sitting on it.

The sharp cawing of crows breaks through my sleep. I open my eyes and see the lake stretching out in front of me, smooth and dark. Rayne is curled up near the firepit, gripping a stick in his hand, sound asleep. Down the beach a deer stands in the shallow water, head tipped forward, quenching its thirst.

The sleeping bag I'm wrapped in is damp. I slip my arm

back inside and feel between my legs. Thank goodness. I have on one of those thick diapers. It's soggy but at least the sleeping bag isn't wet from that. I try to move.

"Lord, help me!" I shout. "I'm paralyzed from the waist down!"

Rayne wakes and jumps to his feet. "What? What's wrong?"

"I can't move. My body's totally seized up," I say.

He sits back in the sand. "Relax. You're just stiff from sleeping on the ground. Take it slowly. Wiggle your toes, bend your knees. You're fine." He folds his arms around bent knees and rests his head on his arms.

I squirm out of the sleeping bag. A car door slams behind me. Audrey totters on the uneven ground.

"You're just stiff, take it slow," I call to her, repeating Rayne's advice.

Rayne stays in the crouched position, head buried.

"Are you okay?" I ask.

"I can't believe I've lost Shadow. What the hell is wrong with me? Everyone who gets close to me ends up gone." His shoulders sag even more. "God, that sounds so pathetic. But it's true: my grandma, my mom, my first dog, my girlfriend, now Shadow. The only one left is my dad and he doesn't seem too happy about seeing me again, either."

"We want you here," I say quietly. "And Shadow isn't gone. She's just missing."

He still doesn't move.

"Listen, young man, you go find that dog. She's probably hiding in the cloakroom or a under a desk, or maybe under the back porch. I don't know, but you'd better find her because I can see that nothing productive is going to get done today until you do."

He looks up at me with a strange softness in his eyes. "I need to get my dog from the cloakroom now," he says, and stands to leave.

Audrey and I wash up with cold water scooped from the lake into a big bowl, in privacy behind a blanket hung over the open car door. It's tricky. Each movement is challenging, but we hold each other up, help fasten bras and maneuver into clean clothes. By the time we're finished, we are exhausted.

We emerge from behind our blanket and Rayne is sitting on the log in his wet undies, looking at the lake. He must have stripped to his boxers and gone for a swim while we were busy.

"We need to bury something. Could you help us dig a hole?" I ask, blushing unexpectedly.

He looks at the yellowed wads of padding we hold behind our backs and cringes. "Oh, that is gross. I'm not touching those." He digs a deep hole away from the water's edge, then walks across the road and into the woods. He calls Shadow's name every few seconds, the voice moving farther and farther away and then gone completely.

Inside the car, doors splayed open, we soak in the fresh air and comfort of soft seats. I pull my notepad out and jot down a few things.

campfire. no Shadow. sand and water. striped blouse. happy.

I tuck the pen inside and set the book down on the seat. "What are we gonna do if Rayne doesn't come out of those roots?" I ask.

"Who?"

"Rayne."

Silence.

"Your boyfriend," I say.

"My boyfriend?" Audrey laughs. "I'm married. What are you talking about?"

"I'm talking about your boyfriend, Rayne, who is driving us somewhere, except that he isn't because he's gone to look for his dog that's lost in the forest over there."

"Do we have anything to eat?"

"Just dog food."

"That's it? Dog food?" Audrey says. "I'm not eating that. Let's go find some real food."

"I don't know. Your boyfriend will be upset if we go for food without him. We should wait a bit longer," I say.

"Nonsense. We'll go and buy some food and bring it back here. We'll be back before he shows up."

"Okay." I move from the backseat to the front and reach for the ignition. "That guy must have the keys," I say. "We'll have to wait for him."

Audrey asks, "Do we have anything to eat?"

"No. We have to wait for your boyfriend to get back."

"I hope he's not long. I'm starving."

10

WE SETTLE INTO the cushioned seats until the sound of someone pounding on the hood of the car startles us.

It's Rayne. He has Shadow in his arms. "Look who I found tangled in the undergrowth."

He walks around to the side of the car and lays Shadow gently down on the blanket that was left in a heap on the sand. The dog just stays there, moving only her head in an effort to keep Rayne in her sight. There are scratches on Shadow's face and bits of clotted blood stuck to her hair everywhere. Her left hind leg has an open wound, the blood still glistening wet but no longer streaming down, as it clearly must have been. She whimpers and makes a feeble attempt at wagging her tail.

"Shh. Quiet, Girl. It's okay." Rayne holds his hand on the side of her belly to soothe her. "It's okay now."

"Lillian," he says. "Could you just stand here and talk to her? Try to keep her still if you can."

I move in beside Shadow. Rayne pulls a T-shirt from his big pack in the trunk and tears it into strips. He pours some water from the jug onto some pieces and cleans the dirt and blood from the wounds. He uses the remaining strips to wrap her back leg securely. Audrey fills the bowl with clean water so Shadow can drink.

"I don't know how badly she's hurt," Rayne says after watching her lap up the water. "She isn't even trying to get up. Her collar was caught on a branch and she must have struggled so hard to get loose, that she got all scratched up. Or maybe she had to defend herself. There's lots of wildlife around here."

I shoot him a look of surprise. "We slept outside. What kind of wildlife?"

"Black bear, moose, deer, fox. That's why I stayed up and kept the fire going until just before dawn. I had it under control."

"I'm glad I slept in the car," Audrey says.

I pat Shadow softly. "Do you think she could defend herself against a bear?"

"No, especially not snagged like that, but she could make a lot of noise and in the dark, that might scare it away." Rayne says.

"Can we go?" Audrey asks. "I'm gonna pass out from starvation."

"Yeah. We need to get moving," Rayne agrees.

We pack everything back into the car, shake out the blanket and shape it into a nest on the seat beside me. Rayne lifts Shadow onto the blanket and she falls asleep before we get back to the highway.

We stop at the first restaurant we see. It has a huge parking lot, big enough to hold dozens of transport trucks and cars. There is only one truck and ours is the only car.

Rayne checks the clock on the dash. "Nine-thirty—too late for truckers to be eating breakfast and too early for morning coffee break. Good timing," he says. "The place isn't busy."

We open the windows a couple of inches and leave Shadow resting in the car. Rayne chooses a table in the corner.

"Why are we sitting way back here? It's so dark. We like to sit by the window," Audrey says.

I wonder the same thing, but a quick glance at Rayne tells me not to challenge him. He looks around at the empty tables, then jumps up, returning with a newspaper left by an earlier diner. "This is how I kept up with the news when I was on the street," he says.

Audrey tries again. "Can we move closer to the window?"

Rayne still doesn't answer. He scans the front page then starts through the sports section. A man approaches the table with a damp cloth and a pot of coffee.

"Morning," He swipes the cloth once across the table. "Coffee?"

He pours before anyone answers, reaches into the pocket of his apron and drops a handful of creamers on the table. "I'll be back to take your orders," he says as he scuffs to his previous spot behind the counter.

Audrey looks for a menu. "I'm hungry. Did I mention that?" she says. "I'm hungry and I don't like sitting here."

I reach over to pat her hand. "We need to get you some food. You're grumpy when you're hungry."

I wave at the man behind the counter, gesturing that we

need menus. He ignores me and continues to scratch away at a lottery ticket he has pulled from another pocket of his apron. Rayne stands, picks up three menus from a tray near the door and passes them out as he sits back down. "I guess it's self-serve."

Audrey hollers across the room. "Excuse me, could you hurry over here and take our orders, or do we have to go to the kitchen and make it ourselves?"

A lone truck driver sitting at another table bursts into loud guffaws. "She's got your number, Sam. It sure didn't take her long to figure out how it works around here."

Sam's only response is to continue to scratch all the boxes on his ticket. When he finishes, he tosses it into the garbage and casually shuffles over to the table. "What can I get you?" he mumbles without looking up.

"I'll have pancakes and bacon and a bowl of prunes," Audrey says. "My bowels could use a kick-start. And don't take all morning with it either. I'm hungry."

"No prunes—peaches. Do you want peaches?"

"Fine. I'll have more coffee too, if it's not too much trouble," she says sarcastically.

Rayne and I order and the man disappears through a swinging door to what must be the kitchen.

"You are one tough cookie, Miss Audrey," I tease.

Audrey shrugs. "I get a little testy before breakfast."

Rayne returns to reading the newspaper. He picks up the City Section and turns to the second page. His eyes open wider and he turns pale. He points to an article and then reads it to us quietly.

"Police suspect foul play as two elderly women disappear from Tranquil Meadows Nursing Home. Police

are widening their search for Lillian Gorsen and Audrey Clark, missing since Wednesday morning from a long-term care facility in Ottawa. These two women suffer from Alzheimer's disease and were last seen at breakfast on Wednesday. Their families are concerned for their safety, stating the women are unable to function on their own. Gorsen's family has offered a reward for her safe return. Police are intensifying their province-wide search and ask anyone with information about the whereabouts of Gorsen and Clark to contact the Ontario Provincial Police immediately."

"That's ridiculous!" Audrey's voice is rising and Rayne frowns, nodding toward other customer. Luckily, Audrey catches his drift. "What do they mean we're unable to function on our own?" she whispers. "We're doing just fine, thank you very much."

Rayne folds the paper and lays it on the table. His hands are shaking, and he looks really stressed.

"I had an ominous feeling last night when I sat there watching the fire," he says. "I convinced myself it was just because I was worried about Shadow, but when I found her, the feeling didn't go away. You have to go to the police and return to the nursing home."

"No! I vote no. Audrey, what do you say?"

"Are you kidding?" Audrey says. "We camped on the beach last night, didn't we? And we stripped down for a sponge bath in the wide-open spaces. And we're eating whatever we want—if that devil-waiter ever brings us our breakfast. I don't want to go back there yet."

I smile. "You heard the lady. We can't go back, at least not yet. I knew I chose the right travel partner."

Rayne clenches his jaw tightly and says nothing more.

Audrey hollers again. "Hey, Sweetheart! Where's our breakfast?"

When we're finished, the waiter tears the bill off his pad and slides it along the table next to Audrey's hand.

She looks up at him. "You sure are handsome, but your manners need a little fine-tuning. We could work on that in the car if you want to join us. We're heading west."

"Nineteen dollars and fifty-five cents—that's what you owe," he says gruffly and walks back through the door to the kitchen.

"Come on," I say. "Let's go before you get us into some kind of trouble with Romeo over there." I leave twenty dollars on the table. Rayne slips the newspaper under his arm and we return to the car.

Shadow tries to stand when she sees us. She is unsteady on her feet, but her tail wags and her eyes look clearer. Rayne lifts her down to the pavement. Wobbly but upright, she makes her way to a patch of weeds off to the side of the lot and pees while Rayne smokes another joint. Shadow slowly limps back to the car, waiting to be hoisted inside.

As we drive away, Rayne turns to Audrey. "It's important that you don't tell people where we're going. Do you understand? We need a plan, or we might as well turn around right now and drive straight back to the nursing home."

Audrey pouts. "I don't know what you're talking about."

"You told that waiter that we're going west," Rayne says. "You can't do that. The police have ordered a province-wide

126

search and everyone who reads the paper is going to be watching. You don't need to make it easier by announcing who you are and where you're going."

Her face wrinkles up and she starts to cry.

"Oh, shit. Stop it. I'm only trying to avoid getting caught. Do you want the police to catch us and send you back?"

"Leave me alone." Audrey sniffles through her tears.

I offer Shadow pieces of dog food one at a time. "Albert's right, Fraise. We need to be more careful. It's important we don't get lost. Albert knows the way. He'll get us there safely, and then we'll send for the kids when they're done school."

Albert glances in the rearview mirror. I catch his eye and wink at him.

"Lillian," he says, looking ahead at the road and then back in the mirror. "I'm not Albert. Stay with me on this."

Why is Albert saying that? He's always kidding around, but this doesn't feel like a joke. I watch the rocky scenery whiz past. Albert must be changing to a new job in British Columbia. He always says that the company is looking for good salespeople out west. I'm glad we're moving, setting out on a new journey. Something behind us has gone awry. I strain to remember what has happened, what we're running from. Maybe later it will come to me.

"The kids will fly out later to join us, right Albert?" I ask.

"I think your kids..." He doesn't finish.

"What are you saying?" I ask. "And don't call them my kids, they're ours, yours and mine. You're their father."

Albert ignores me and talks to Fraise. "We just need to keep a low profile. The less contact you and Lillian have with others, the better. For now, you two need to be invisible."

"Like superheroes?" Fraise asks.

"Yeah, invisible superheroes."

I stroke Shadow's head again and again and watch the world speed by the window. I try again. Maybe this time Albert and Fraise will understand.

"Are we moving?" I ask.

Albert's edgy, a little impatient now. "We're in the car, and the car is moving. Is that what you're asking?"

"No, and don't patronize me. Are we moving to a new house?"

"Lillian, when this started, you said it was a vacation. I'm not sure what you want to call it now. Do you want to keep going or go back?"

"Fraise, what do you think? You are coming to stay with us, right? I think we should let Fraise decide where we should live, don't you, Albert?"

Silence.

"Jeez Louise! Why won't anyone answer me?"

I scratch behind the dog's ears, rubbing a bit too close to a scrape on her face and causing her to flinch. I look more closely and see that the dog has a dressing wrapped around her leg. "What's wrong, Puppy?" I say as I gently rub my finger under her chin, then scoop a few pebbles of dog food from the bowl on the floor and offer them to her.

"Blondie's hurt," I say. "Her leg is bandaged, and she has cuts all over her."

Again no one answers. It's like there is a soundproof wall between the front and back seat. This invisible quiet-wall will come in handy next time I'm driving with Tom and Carol arguing in the back.

"Well, Girl," I say to the dog, "Looks like we're on our own." I sing the chorus of "How Much is That Doggy in the Window." She sleeps in her blanket-nest. "You rest, little Blondie. You've got some healing to do."

The road is getting busier. Signs say that Highway 11 has merged with Highway 17. Huge trucks pass, carrying enormous tree trunks stacked like oranges in a supermarket. There are more cars too and more exits that lead to places called Red Rock, Hurkett, Dorian, and Sleeping Giant Provincial Park. Reading the road signs and paying attention to details like this makes me feel calmer. There is a sign that tells of a memorial dedicated to Terry Fox and we can see his larger-than-life statue just off to the side.

"He was so strong, running all that way with one leg," Audrey says.

"Who was he?" I ask.

"Don't you remember Terry Fox? I remember when he ran through Ottawa and everyone went out to see him. He was a hero. I watched him shake hands with Trudeau," Audrey says.

I wonder who Trudeau was and why he was shaking hands with this statue.

We turn at an exit and stop at a large grocery store. No one pays any attention to us as we move up and down the aisles.

"Let's get a Styrofoam cooler and some ice, so we can buy more food and not have to keep stopping," Rayne says.

We wander through the store, tossing things into the cart: cold cuts, cheese, juice, buns, bananas, pears, and a package of cookies. At the cash register, I leaf through the money in my wallet and count it out into the cashier's palm. I stop just short of the thirty-five dollars showing on the screen.

"That's all I have. Do you have money?" I ask Audrey.

"I don't know where my purse is," she says, looking around.

Rayne pulls some small bills from his pocket and pays the rest.

"Damn!" he says as we return to the car. "We're gonna need more cash. The problem is they can track you if you use your credit or debit card. We're short on gas too."

"Who can track us?" I ask.

"The bank, your family, the nursing home."

"You mean they'll know where we are because we take money out of the bank this far away?" I say.

"Yeah. Everything's electronic."

"Even the credit cards? Would they know right away if we used the credit card too?" I can picture the bank teller pouring over bank entries, noting every transaction that every customer makes across the country.

"They might have flagged your accounts to notify them if any action takes place," Rayne explains.

"This is much more complicated than I thought," Audrey says. "It's hard to run away from home."

Rayne pulls up in front of an automated bank machine nearby. "We can't go any farther without gas. We're gonna have to take a chance. Do either of you have a credit card?"

Audrey shakes her head. "Did I leave my purse somewhere?"

I find a bankcard in my wallet that Rayne says will probably work. With Rayne's help, I insert it into the slot. The screen lights up and asks for the PIN number. I turn to Rayne and shrug.

"Try this," he says, reaching across and touching the

keys 1-2-3-4. The screen goes black and then, *Incorrect PIN. Cancel or retry.*

"What about the last four digits of your phone number?"

"1455. I'm sure that was our number at home, wasn't it, Fraise?" I say.

He punches that into the keypad. Incorrect PIN. Cancel or retry.

This is kind of fun, like a guessing game. "What about my birthday? Try that."

"When's your birthday?" Rayne asks.

"February 26."

He touches the keys 0-2-2-6. The screen changes and asks what action I want to take. Rayne quickly presses the withdraw option. "How much can we get?" he asks. "Is a thousand too much?"

"Go ahead and try it," I say. "I guess we'll see."

The machine whirs and beeps, and a wad of bills appears in a tray at the bottom.

"Well, look at that!" Audrey can barely get the words out. "That's unbelievable. Who knew you could get one thousand dollars just by putting your card in a machine and pushing the right numbers?" She laughs. "One thousand dollars. We're set."

Rayne hands the money to me but keeps some. "I'll need this for gas," he says.

"Good job. What a team," I say. "That was easy enough, eh?"

We drive away in search of a gas station. Rayne's voice is heavy. "It was simple enough, but I have a feeling it's gonna cause problems for us in the very near future."

Rayne fills the tank, and we head west, accelerating onto the highway past several more exits that lead into Thunder Bay. Just outside the city, he veers onto a side road.

"I've got an idea," he says.

11

"WHAT IS IT, DEAR?" Audrey asks.

"I've been wired up about this stolen car situation and expecting to get pulled over any minute by the police. We've been gone three days now. We're pushing our luck, but I have an idea."

Rayne is bouncy, tapping his fingers on the steering wheel, more childlike than I've seen him before. He's talking so quickly, I'm having trouble understanding. "We need to clean up the Intrigue, so there's no trace of us anywhere inside or outside, and leave it somewhere safe, like outside a police station. Then we need to rent a car. No one has connected the two of you with me, so I could go alone to the rental place, use cash, then pick you up, and we can drive the rest of the way in the rental. As long as we clean the Intrigue up really well before deserting it, it shouldn't lead anyone to think you're the ones who took it."

"I'm not sure I understand," Audrey says. "If they find the car in Thunder Bay, won't they know we're here?"

"Not as long as there's nothing in it to connect you. Anyone could have stolen it and left it here. I'll take it to a carwash, scrub it, and then vacuum inside."

The surface changes to gravel a short distance off the highway. We creep slowly along. Rayne looks left and right, searching for something, I'm not sure what. He spots a lane that leads into the trees.

The wheels turn silently as they roll along a dirt path that opens up to a frame house with broken windows. The paint is so faded it's impossible to tell what color it was. Rayne turns off the engine and jumps from the car. He disappears behind the house and a few minutes later, reappears on the opposite side. He saunters over and opens the car door. His face is beaming.

"No one around. Perfect." He leans in closer. "Okay, here's the deal. We'll unload everything onto the porch. You stay here with Shadow. I'll drive into the city, go to a carwash, and then park the Intrigue on the street across from a police station. I'll find a car rental place and come back here to pick you up."

He looks so happy with himself. "What do you think of my plan?"

My heart is beating faster. "Delicious!" I say. "Can I come with you?"

"I need you to stay here with Audrey and Shadow and all our stuff," Rayne says. "I will need some money, though, for the carwash and the rental."

"Do we have to get rid of my car?" Audrey asks.

"If things work out the way I hope, it'll be returned safely to the boy you borrowed it from, and we'll be able to go the rest of the way without being charged with theft—a good deal if you ask me," Rayne says.

I slide out of the car, followed by Shadow who slinks gingerly down from the seat with a squeal.

"Can you put the leash on her?" Rayne says, handing it to me. "I don't want to take any chances."

I hook the leash onto Shadow's collar and Rayne ties it securely to a rung on the porch railing. Audrey leans on her cane and drags her bag to the porch. Rayne does most of the lifting and carrying: the guitar, backpacks, dog food, his big sleeping bag, the blanket, and the cooler filled with food.

"We should have lunch before you go," Audrey says. "We haven't eaten yet today."

"What about breakfast with your friend Sam, the world's worst waiter?" Rayne teases.

He takes a sandwich and banana and waves good-bye. "When you see me next time, I'll be driving a minivan or whatever goes for the cheapest rate and still has room for three people, a dog and luggage. Audrey—Lillian—whatever happens, do *not* leave this place." He waits for us to acknowledge this and then drives away.

The Intrigue disappears at the end of the lane, swallowed up by a cloud of dust. We listen from the front porch as the crunch of gravel under the tires grows quiet and the sounds of isolation engulf us. Crickets and frogs chirp, and birds call to each other in the trees. It feels like there isn't another person for miles in any direction.

"This sandwich is heavenly," Audrey says.

I fill a bowl with water from the jug and another with

kibble and place them where Shadow can reach. She laps up the water with great enthusiasm.

Audrey and I scan the property from our perch on the front steps. The yard isn't really a lawn but more of a meadow, any manicured portions long-since choked out by wildflowers and weeds. Sumac trees grow close to the house, brushing against the wooden clapboard siding and sprouting up randomly between dandelions, chicory, and rocks.

The porch is wooden, gray with age but solid. I reach back to the pile of things that Rayne has stashed there from the car, pull the sleeping bag over and spread it out, then slowly, carefully, lie flat on my back.

Audrey lies down beside me, inhaling sharply as she rolls onto her bruised hip, then she sighs. "Aaaah, that feels great."

"You said it."

The sun warms like a wonderful massage. It's so peaceful here. I waver between sleep and wakefulness until the sound of a car speeding along the road draws me back. We each try to sit up, squirm around like sea lions and finally, raise our heads in time to see a flash of red fly right on by the lane, followed by the billowing gray-white puff that settles along the roadside.

"Rayne is coming back, right?" I ask.

"He'll be back, don't worry," Audrey says.

Rayne has left us here. He's gone on without us. He has our car and he knows how to get money from my bank.

This time, I manage to push and pull myself to a seated position and help Audrey do the same. "Oh, my God!" I say. "We are such trusting old birds. We're in the middle of nowhere—we don't even know where—and we have no way to get back."

"What are you talking about?" Audrey says. "Rayne is coming back for us."

"No, he isn't. He just took off without us, and we let him go. When did we turn so stupid? I knew this was a bad idea, letting him come along in the first place."

"Settle down, my friend. He is coming back."

"Oh, really? You can predict the future now?"

"Why would he drive away and leave us here?"

I frantically try to plan how we will survive. "He left the food and the bags at least. That shows he isn't planning to come back for us. He left the sleeping bag and blanket."

"He left the dog too. He wouldn't do that if he wasn't coming back. He loves that dog," Audrey says.

"I don't know."

"He left the dog so she would protect us until he got back, I bet," Audrey says.

"We need to make a plan," I say, standing with the help of the railing.

"He's adorable," Audrey says.

"Who? The dog?"

"No. Rayne. I like him."

"Oh, he's a prince all right. We'll see how much you like him when he doesn't come back."

"I wish he was my son. I always wanted a son, and he'd be perfect."

"He's yours then," I say.

"Thank you. You're a good friend."

I cross the porch to look in the window, one of the only ones left intact. The room is empty, the wooden floor is stained from weather that found its way inside. Yellowed wallpaper clings to the walls and drapes loosely from the corners—melting.

"I suppose we could fix this place up and live here," I say. "You and me and our dog. It could be beautiful with a little love and elbow grease."

"Help me up this step so I can see," Audrey says, holding her cane in one hand and reaching for me with the other.

I test the railing's strength, then hold on tightly. We teeter together until Audrey tips forward and releases her grasp. She manages to balance herself. Her hand lands flat on the porch floor.

I spin around and grab the railing with both hands, saving myself from going down.

My arms are shaky. "Whew. That was close!" I say. "We're gonna need to have a ramp put in there instead of the step. And a good, sturdy handrail."

Audrey is on her butt, winded and laughing. "Or a trampoline."

"We could have a big garden to grow all our own food," I say.

Audrey clasps her hands together and looks out through the trees. "I could make all the curtains and start my own dressmaking business and popcorn stand."

"I love popcorn," I say, "with lots of butter and Scotch. Do you really think Rayne is coming back?"

"Oh, he'll be back," Audrey says. "What about Terry though?"

I try to remember who Terry is.

"He's not coming back. He died. I forget sometimes, but I know. He died."

I bow my head, "God rest his soul. Terry and Albert, gone to a better place."

"Do you like emerald?" Audrey asks, "Because I could make emerald curtains. I always loved emerald. It sounds like Ireland and jewelry and candy."

"I like azure. Wait, I think it's azule. In all the romantic books and movies the sea and sky are always azure, or azule," I say. "Could I have blue curtains in my bedroom?"

Blue curtains. I had blue-green curtains in that place we left behind. They were heavy and suffocating. I can feel the weight of them closing around me as I stand on the porch.

"I want yellow curtains," I say. "I want yellow curtains, and I don't care if your son comes back to get us. I'm going to stay here anyway. If you want to go with him, just go ahead. I'll be fine."

"He is coming back, and we can all live here. There's room for him too. I'll give him the blue curtains," Audrey says.

"Do you like the uniforms?" I ask.

"Sure, they're pretty nice. I like that little one with the ponytail. She always gives me hugs and calls me Cutie. You know the one?"

"No. They call us Cutie and Hon because they don't know our names. That's why. Just like that dunderhead my mom married. Called me Kiddo all the time because he couldn't bother to sort out which one of us was which. 'Hey, Kiddo. Put some ice and a couple ounces of whiskey in this glass for me, will you?' Do it yourself, Asshole. That's what I should have said, but Mom would have tanned my hide."

"You really think they don't know our names?" Audrey asks.

"Mm-hmm, and I think they're trying to get rid of us.

They give us all those pills—a hundred a day. What are they for, do you ever wonder that? We're not taking any now, and we haven't gone crazy yet. You have to ask yourself what those pills really do."

"I never thought of that," Audrey says. "I'm not going to take mine anymore. When we get back, I'm gonna hide them in my shoe and then throw them down the toilet."

We sit on the steps and wait. "Do you know my mom's second husband, Stuart?" I ask.

"No," Audrey says. "I don't like him though. He sounds like a nasty man. Why is your mom married to him?"

"I don't know. He never even pretended to like us kids from the start. We all begged Mom not to marry him. She said he would look after us. Provide for us. I was thirteen, and the war was just coming to an end. It must have been…1945. I knew we didn't have much. We wore hand-me-downs and ate bread pudding a lot. I remember Mom waiting for the new Family Allowance money to come every month. Still, I couldn't believe she would marry that man. I practically turned myself inside out; cried for days and nights when Mom told us. I threw my framed picture of Humphrey Bogart and Ingrid Bergman at her. The glass broke and cut her arm. I didn't even feel bad, except I really liked that picture."

"You should live with me," Audrey says.

"Susie and Sharon moved out as soon as they had the chance. One or another of my brothers was always threatening to beat the daylights out of Stuart, but they just ended up moving out too. Now there's just John and me at home. I've been thinking of leaving too, but I have nowhere to go."

"But you do. We can all live here. Remember?"

Shadow lifts her head and barks. The telltale dust veil drifts up from the road as a white van slows out front and turns into the lane. Rayne hops out, a big smile on his face.

"I'm glad you're still here," he says. "What do you think of our new wheels?"

"Where have you been?" I ask. "I thought you weren't coming back."

"I went to get the new vehicle. How do you like it?"

Audrey looks around. "Where's the car?"

"This is our new car," Rayne says. "It has more room and lots of tinted windows so you can see out, but people can't see in. It's the Grand Caravan. It's cheap to rent, gets pretty good mileage, and best of all, it's not stolen."

"Where's the Intrigue?" Audrey insists.

"It's sitting across from a police station waiting for someone to notice the plates and return it to your neighbor. Don't worry, it's all good, Audrey," Rayne says.

He opens the rear door and starts loading our baggage.

"We're going to live here," I say. "You can just move that stuff right inside the house instead."

"No, we need to keep moving," he says, continuing to load the minivan. "We're almost to Manitoba."

"Manitoba? Really?" Audrey's eyebrows shoot up and she struggles to her feet. "I've never been there."

"Well let's go then," Rayne says. "It should be four or five hours to Kenora, just this side of the Manitoba border. It's about two-fifteen. We can get there before dark if we leave now."

We fold down the seat beside mine and settle Shadow onto the blanket. With everything stowed, we head back out along Highway 17.

"This is great," Audrey says. "I can see everything sitting up here. It's like being in a big truck."

Shadow licks the small wounds on her front legs, stopping only to check that her travel companions are all still here.

There is a guitar case in the back. "Do you play the guitar?"

"Yeah, I play and sing. That's what I was hoping to do with my life, but now I'm not sure."

"What do you mean?" I ask.

"It's not so easy making a living as a musician. I moved east to play with a band in Montreal, then they broke up and I found studio work in Toronto. I played some backups here and there and a few gigs on my own in Ottawa. That was good for a while, but it's expensive to travel all the time and keep an apartment. Work's hard to find too, sometimes."

"It sounds exciting. You need to keep trying to make it work."

"I miss playing. I've barely picked up my guitar since we left Ottawa. I was thinking that if I can't find enough work back home, maybe I'll try teaching or something for a while."

"You can teach me," I say.

Audrey is asleep. The van rides smoothly, quietly, filled with the new-car scent of carpet and upholstery not yet smudged by pet smells or coffee spills. I spot my notebook poking out of my purse. I write:

yellow curtains. money from machine. guitar lessons. van

Outside the window, the world blurs past. Book and pen still on my lap, I can feel myself nodding off.

Late afternoon. The light in the sky is changing and Rayne has turned on the radio. Music drifts faintly from the speakers.

"Can we stop soon?" I ask.

Audrey is awake now too. "I'm so stiff you might have to just give me a shove and let me topple down from this seat," she says.

We pass exits to Dryden. The signs fly past the windows. "Rayne, I have to stop now."

"All right, relax," he says as he turns into a truck stop restaurant. "Remember, inconspicuous. In fact, don't use your real names, just in case. I'm afraid there might be new information about you being in the area since you used your credit card in Thunder Bay."

"Can I still be Lucy?" I ask.

"Just don't make a scene."

"I have to go now. Can we get the stories straight after I go to the bathroom?" I ask. I wrestle with the door. "How do I get out of this contraption?"

Rayne jumps out and opens my door from the outside. "Go. We'll wait here."

I hurry as fast as I can across the parking lot, find a washroom and rush in, focused on the cubicles on the other side of the room.

"Hey, Lady, this is the men's room."

I glance up to see a man, tucking and zipping in front of a urinal. "Don't worry. I've seen it all before," I say, rushing to the closest stall.

"What the hell?" the man mutters as he opens the door to leave. "You can't even get away from women in the can."

As I leave, I come face-to-face with a policeman. He turns and checks the symbol on the door, then looks back at me.

"Excuse me, Ma'am. This is the men's room," he says politely.

"Thank you, Dear. My mistake. Forgive me." I remember Rayne's warning and add, "My name is Lucy."

The officer smiles and nods uncomfortably. I return to the van, proud that I remembered to cover my tracks.

Shadow shows a little more zest as the day passes. We drive on for another hour. Dusk is falling as we turn off the highway to find a place to stay on the outskirts of Kenora. The sky is hidden behind massive charcoal clouds and raindrops are just beginning to splat onto the windshield. We pull into the Pines Motel.

Rayne's eyes are rimmed with fatigue as he slides from the van.

"I'll be right back," he says. "I'll tell them I need a room for my grandma and aunt, like before, and one for me. Try to keep Shadow out of sight."

Rayne enters the motel office and returns soon after with two room keys. "Perfect—they took the cash, had a look at my driver's license and the license plate—done. Simple. I love having the rental. It makes life so much easier." He unlocks the doors to adjacent rooms. The rain is coming down in a heavy drizzle now, forming huge puddles in the parking lot.

"I'm toast. I think I'll turn in and try to catch up on my sleep," Rayne says. He unloads the packs and his guitar and sneaks Shadow past the *no pets* sign posted just inside the room.

"You need to keep quiet, Girl," I hear him say as he disappears inside.

I am wide awake. Audrey and I freshen up, have a bite to eat from the food stashed in the cooler, then look out into the darkness. The rain has stopped and droplets glow like fireflies on the branches as the lights from the window and the full moon reflect off them.

"It looks like tinsel on a Christmas tree," Audrey says.

"Christmas will be here before we know it, and I haven't bought the kids anything yet. Time slips by so fast, I just can't keep up anymore."

"I have some money. We can shop tomorrow if you want," Audrey says. "I'm gonna buy something for Rayne."

I look around the room. The curtains and bedspreads are in matching shades of drab turquoise. What is it with that color? It's everywhere I go. The place is clean enough. In fact, it has a slightly antiseptic smell but just feels uncomfortable, if oddly familiar. It is small and except for the large lamp by the window, sort of dim. Why is this room having this effect on me? I glance at the clock. Eleven-thirty. Late, but I'm not ready to go to sleep.

"I'm not tired. I'm going for a walk," I announce. "Do you want to come with me?"

Audrey rubs her hip. "Just a short walk? My leg is sore, but it could be from sitting so much. The exercise might do me some good."

12

WE PULL ON SWEATERS and shoes and start out the door. Audrey notices the room key on the desk. "We better take the key so we can get back in."

"What if we lose it? We should leave it here," I say.

"But we won't be able to get in."

"We'll leave the door unlocked. We won't be long," I say. "Here, just put this book in the door so it doesn't close all the way." I wedge the local business directory in the doorframe.

The air is so fresh, wild, flushed from the end-of-day rainstorm. It's warm—mid-August I think—and the full moon shines in all the puddles and leaves and along the strip of pavement that leads away from the motel. We plod steadily along the road, listening to the sounds of traffic on the highway a short distance away. We walk in the opposite direction. The silence balloons around us.

"We should turn around," Audrey says. "We better not

go too far, or we might get lost. Besides, I'm getting tired."

"Just smell that," I say, ignoring Audrey. "It's so big and clean." We come upon a driveway carved through the trees. "Look, Audrey. It's our house." I turn into the lane and pick my way carefully toward the house at the end of the drive. Audrey follows, cautious of her footing on the muddy ground. The porch light shines blue, just bright enough to illuminate the front of the house but not the surrounding property. Two worn wicker rocking chairs sit on either side of a rustic twig table. The chairs have high backs and thick cushions covered in bright fabric. Inside the house it's dark and quiet.

"Can we just rest for a minute before we walk back?" Audrey whispers.

I smile. "We can do whatever we want. Let's sit."

We drop down into the soft seats and rock back and forth in this private paradise making a quiet, creaking rhythm on the wooden floor.

I awaken at dawn to the laughter of small children. With eyes closed, I delight in the giggles. But these are my small children, playing unsupervised somewhere while I doze carelessly. I look around at the gardens, the tricycles and swing set in the yard, and at Fraise, sleeping in the chair beside me. I try to stand, but pain stabs through my back. I try again, manage to rise partway and turn around to face the house. Behind a large window, a curious young woman peers out at me. The laughter has stopped and there are two children peeking out from behind this lady's back.

I sit down in the chair.

The woman opens the door and peers out. Fraise opens

her eyes and lets out a raspy scream, but doesn't move from her seat next to mine.

The woman rallies her boys back from the door and tells them to stay inside, then steps out onto the porch, scanning the yard. She wears a knee-length, blue nightgown with embroidered yellow flowers and speaks in a gentle voice, like a kindergarten teacher on the first day of school.

"Can I help you?" she asks, looking around the yard again as if expecting a crowd of people to emerge from the bushes.

I gather the thoughts from their jumbled place inside my head. "Fraise and I, we thought this was our house. We fell asleep."

Fraise speaks up. "Ethel. I'm Ethel and this is Lucy."

I continue, "I thought I heard my children laughing. Where are Tom and Carol? Do you know?"

The young woman can see her boys through the screen door. She moves closer to me. "Is it your grandchildren you're looking for? Are you lost? I can help you."

Fraise answers. "I think we are lost. Do you have anything to eat?"

I can't believe that Fraise is worried about eating when the kids are missing. Before the woman can answer, I ask again, my voice rising in pitch. "Do you know where Tom and Carol are? I heard them laughing."

The woman kneels in front of me. "I'm Susan. I live here, and the children you heard were my two sons, Travis and Trevor. I don't know where your children are, but maybe I can help you find them."

She talks slowly as if calculating each phrase. I can sense she is sincere and wants to help.

She looks down the driveway and around the yard. "How did you get here?"

I only remember waking up in this chair.

Fraise shrugs and scratches her head. She looks down at her shoes. They are covered in dried mud. "I think we must have walked."

Susan turns back toward the door. "While we figure this out, I'm going to make you a pot of tea and some toast. Will you wait here?" She raises her eyebrows in a pleading expression, a look that says she is unsure we'll still be there when she returns.

When the woman has gone, Fraise leans over, bringing her face close to mine. "Lillian, are you okay? You're very quiet."

My eyes feel like they're coated in a translucent film. "I'm losing things—not things—not things you can hold in your hand. It's scary."

She reaches for my hand, then rises from her chair with grunts and groans and moves closer. "It's gonna be fine, Honey. We're almost to Manitoba."

We hear water running in the kitchen and the kettle clattering on the stove. The television is switched on and cartoon voices and songs dance out through the screen door. I feel like I am someone else watching all of this from some other place. It all seems far away.

Susan returns to the porch, carrying a tray that she sets on the table. She hands us each a plate of toast with jam and pours three cups of tea. The two little boys follow her, one balancing a plate of apple wedges and the other, squares of cheese. She leans against the railing and looks back and forth at her two unexpected guests. The sun is just beginning to show from around the side of the house.

"Now then, what are your names again?"

Fraise repeats the names she has practiced over and over in her head. "Lucy and Ethel."

I watch her as she says these and repeat them to hear how they sound coming from my mouth. "Lucy and Ethel." They're familiar, and so I let them rest there.

"Okay," Susan says. "Lucy, Ethel, do you live around here?"

I look at Fraise for the answer. "No," she says, hesitantly. "We're going to British Columbia." She stops and scratches her head again. Her eyes return to the mud on her shoes. She moves her cane and notices that it, too, is muddy an inch or so up the shaft. She looks back at Susan and smiles. "We walked here last night."

I hear the words but do not grasp their meaning. I replay the names in my head—Audrey, Fraise, Ethel, Lucy. I can't place exactly who this woman is, sitting beside me with such natural intimacy. She must be Ethel.

She has clearly started to relax as she continues with her story. "We went for a walk last night and thought this was our house. I guess we fell asleep and stayed all night. What a great vacation we're having. Each day it's something new."

The two little boys plop down in front of our chairs.

"Did you know we're twins?" one of them asks.

"Yeah, we were born on the same day and we have the same birthday every year," the other says. "We're four."

"I like trucks. My daddy's a truck driver."

"*I* like trucks," the other boy says, as if only one of them can have that favorite as his own. "You're copying me."

"I like trucks too," Ethel says. "Our new car is like a truck. I can see everything from way up there."

One of the little boys takes hold of Ethel's hand and tugs. "Do you want to go on the swings? Come on, you can push me."

"Travis, Honey, be careful. Maybe Ethel doesn't want to push you on the swings right now," Susan says.

"No, that sounds like fun," Ethel says. "Just give me a minute to get moving, Sweetheart. I'm a little slow."

She follows him to the swing set. Trevor sits on the porch, munching on cheese.

"They are so adorable," I say to Susan.

"They don't get to see their grandparents much," she says. "They live in Nova Scotia. I'm glad you stopped in."

She is so kind to us. I can see that she's glad to have company but still curious about who we are and why we're here. I am feeling the same.

"I'm glad too," I say. "You and your children are very nice. Thank you for everything."

Trevor eases up onto my lap. "Don't go yet. We can play Go Fish. We know how."

I recognize the card game. We play it sometimes at the nursing home. It is one of the games I can play without getting lost, at least most of the time.

"Why don't you go and play on the swings with Travis and Ethel?" Susan says. "I need to talk to Lucy for a minute."

She sits beside me in the other chair. "Now, can you tell me how you got here? Is there anyone else with you?" she asks.

We did walk here. That is clear to me, but I can't remember for the life of me where we walked from, so I try to fake it. "We do have a car and we must be staying nearby. We just got lost and decided to stay here where it felt safe until morning. It was really dark last night. There weren't any stars."

"Sounds frightening. I'm glad you weren't alone."

"Me too," I say. "My friend and I, we should really get going. You must have lots to do. We'll be on our way. I'm sure our car is just on the road somewhere near here. Thank you for everything."

"Nonsense. I'm not sending you off like that. We'll go together. Just give me a minute to get dressed and we'll take a little walk. Please wait here." She looks at me like she is studying a puzzle. "Is there someone we should call to let them know you're safe?"

"No. There's no one. Just us."

"You're sure?"

"Absolutely. We're on vacation. Just two friends on vacation."

"Wait here. Promise?"

I nod. This lady cares about us. I don't really want to leave.

Out in the yard, Ethel has squeezed herself onto the empty swing between the two boys. The three of them swing lazily back and forth in a synchronized dance.

With Susan, we walk to the end of the lane, one little munchkin holding Ethel's hand, the other holding mine.

Susan looks up and down the road. "I don't see your car," she says. "Are you staying at the motel down the road?"

We walk a long way before coming to the motel.

Audrey points at a door propped ajar. "Remember? We left the key inside so we wouldn't lose it."

"Is one of these vehicles yours, then?" Susan asks.

"Yep. Would you like to come in and see our room?" Ethel asks. The boys run to the door and push it open.

"I think I would like to come in for a moment, if you don't mind," Susan says. I can tell she's still nervous about leaving us alone.

Ethel follows the children inside and tells them they can jump on the bed if they want. Susan says they'd better not.

"Is there anyone with you?" she asks again.

Ethel answers. "Rayne is in the room next door. He's my son and he's driving us out west."

"Do you think I could meet him?" Susan asks.

"Sure. Come on, I'll introduce you to him." Ethel leads the way to the room beside ours and knocks. "Rayne," she calls out. "Rayne, it's Audrey. Come and meet our new friends."

Shadow barks from within. A few minutes pass and Rayne comes to the door. He opens it a crack and peers out, red-eyed and scruffy-haired. "Hold on. I'll be right out."

He smells of beer and smoke.

"Open up," Audrey says. "We want you to meet Susan and the little sweeties."

"I'll be out in a minute." His voice is gruff. He shuts the door.

Susan looks worried. She says the name Audrey out loud but nothing more; watches us closely as we wait. Finally, Rayne opens the door just wide enough to edge out. He has Shadow on the leash. "Sorry. I must have overslept," he says. He looks everywhere but at our faces.

Audrey is undeterred. "Rayne, this is Susan and these are her sons. Aren't they handsome?" She puts her arms around the boys' shoulders. "I told Susan that you're my son, and that you are driving us on our vacation."

"Hey," he mumbles. "Nice to meet you."

Susan keeps her gaze on Rayne's face and speaks, straight-forward and firm. "It looks like you've had a rough night."

"I'm fine, not that it's any of your business," he says.

I'm suddenly very cold. Why is he acting like this?

"Hey, hey...don't talk like that," Audrey says. "What's gotten into you?"

"I don't appreciate your friend's insinuation," Rayne says. "Sorry." He directs Shadow back into the room and nods toward Audrey and me. "Get your things together, and we'll leave in a few minutes." Then to Susan, "Look, I'm just a little over-sensitive first thing in the morning. I appreciate your concern."

The door closes behind him.

Susan takes my hand. "Is that really Ethel's...Audrey's son?"

I try to laugh, to put her mind at ease, but it sounds fake, even to me. "Of course. He probably went out last night and had a couple of drinks, but he's not a boozer or anything. He's a nice guy who just wakes up crabby sometimes. We're fine. Thank you for everything."

She slips back into our room and writes her phone number on a piece of paper. She hands it to me. "Please call me if you're in danger." She hugs both of us and the boys do the same. I almost start to cry.

Audrey and I wait in our room in silence. My stomach flips and churns, and I feel like I'm going to throw up.

Some time later, Rayne comes in. "Who was that?" he asks. "Where did you meet her?"

I don't answer. I gather my things and move toward the door.

"Before you go out there, I just want to warn you that

an old friend is joining us," he says. "She needs a ride into town." He pauses. "Um, I need some cash too. Can you lend me a hundred? I'll pay you back when we see an ATM."

My shoulders are numb and my head is pounding. I hand him my purse and he takes out some bills.

A young girl comes out of Tom's room. She's wearing jeans and a black sweatshirt. A gigantic gray purse is slung over her shoulder. Red hair spills from under the hood that she pulls over her head as she walks toward us.

"Mornin'," she says, then casts an awkward look at Tom.

He responds by wordlessly handing her some money and then taking his place behind the wheel. Audrey and the girl both make a move for the front passenger seat.

"Excuse me," Audrey says, pushing past. She climbs up and fastens her seatbelt, assuring her place up front.

The girl backs away and waits until I'm comfortable before easing into the seat beside me. She forces the heavy bag between her feet.

It is like being in church—quiet, all eyes forward as we drive. I can't stand it any longer.

"What's your name?" I ask.

"Chelsea."

"Chelsea, like the buns. Chelsea, Dear, how long have you known Tom?"

She squirms a bit and brushes her fingers through the strands of hair around her face. "We just met."

"Really? And you stayed overnight with him?"

She doesn't answer.

"Very brave. You don't really know a man until you've slept with him. You might as well get that out of the way,

I guess. Now you've met the real Tom, what do you think? Is he trustworthy?"

Tom catches my eye in the rearview mirror but doesn't say anything. Chelsea just looks at me like I have two heads.

"Because we trust him, but I feel like we need a second opinion. You see, we don't have the kind of insight you have."

"Jeezus, Lillian," Tom says. "Be quiet."

"Now there, you see what I mean? We give him everything, and he talks to us like that. What do think of a boy who talks to an old lady like that?"

Chelsea sits up straighter. "I think you're right. That's not very nice."

We turn into the downtown and pull up beside a curb. The girl slides down and out of the van without so much as a wave. As the door glides closed, she hurries away.

Tom drives on, and once again we are in church.

"If I didn't know better, I'd wonder who raised such a rude young man," I say. "How did you turn out like this? Your father would be very disappointed in you right now."

Audrey watches the scenery fly past, apparently unburdened by the change in Tom's temperament. Suddenly she claps her hands and announces, "The Manitoba border. We're crossing into Manitoba. There's an information place. Can we stop and ask for information?"

"We're just gonna keep going," Tom says. He looks straight ahead.

Audrey twists in her seat as far as she can to look at me. "Are you crying?" she asks. "What's wrong? We're in Manitoba, aren't you happy about that? Look! Highway 1."

I can't bring myself to smile, though I want to act like

everything is all right. Like Audrey. She just doesn't seem to notice things. Doesn't she hear him, see him? I get that he is young. I do remember, sometimes vividly, what it's like to have a sex drive. But he talked to us like we were children. "Get your things. Be quiet."

He is starting to make me nervous.

13

THIS ROAD GOES ON forever. A sign points toward Steinbach. The name is vaguely familiar, like the name of a classmate whose face can't be conjured up, or a story recently heard, the details of which are just out of reach.

"Are we going to Steinbach?" I ask.

"No, we're almost to Winnipeg though," Rayne says.

"It didn't take long to get through Ontario," Audrey says. "I feel like we just left home yesterday."

"I feel like we've been driving forever," Rayne says. "But now that we're in Manitoba, it's starting to feel more like home." He eases a bit more comfortably down into the seat. "I should phone my dad tonight. We haven't talked for a long time. I should let him know I'm coming home."

"Will you tell him about us?" I ask.

"No. It would be hard to explain this to someone who's never met you."

"I'm not sure how to take that," Audrey says, "but I think it's good that you let your parents know you're safe and that you're going home."

We cross the Red River Floodway and then the river itself, its water flowing lazily between the banks. After stopping for sandwiches, we drive on toward Brandon. Rayne looks happy, his elbow resting on the frame of the open window, shoulders relaxed, and foot a little heavy on the gas pedal.

From behind, we hear the scream of a siren. Rayne checks the side mirror and eases his foot off the pedal. His face pales as he realizes the sirens are intended for him. He steers the van to the shoulder. The white, unmarked police car follows.

"Don't say a word unless he asks you a question, and if he does, then only answer yes or no. Don't tell him anything," he says.

An officer approaches the window. Rayne pulls the rental papers from the glove compartment and looks up into eyes that glare down from under the brimmed hat of a giant.

"Good afternoon, Sir," Rayne says.

"Afternoon. Could I see your license, please?" the officer says. He leans over and tips his head just inside the window, eyes slowly scanning the interior.

Shadow lurches across the seat and growls. "Quiet, Girl," Rayne says, his elbow blocking her from the front seat. "These are the papers for the rented van." He hands them out the window. "I need to get my driver's license from my pack in the back." He points toward the rear of the van.

The officer steps away from the door to let him out, one hand holding the rental papers, the other hovering near his hip. "Where are you headed?"

Shadow barks and tries to jump to the back of the van as Rayne moves to the rear and opens the door. I listen carefully.

"I'm driving my grandma and aunt to see my dad in B.C." He finds his license and hands it to the officer.

"Wayne Carpenter? Your license says you live in Ottawa, but the lease agreement says you rented the car in Thunder Bay."

"Yeah, we got a ride to Thunder Bay with a friend and then we rented the vehicle there to go the rest of the way."

"Do you know how fast you were going with your grandmother in the car?" he asks.

"Not exactly," Rayne answers.

"Twenty-two clicks over the speed limit. You need to slow down, young man. Here in Manitoba we take speeding seriously."

"Yes, Sir. I understand. I'll be more careful." Rayne bows his head in hopes that he'll get off with a warning.

"You're driving your grandma and aunt all the way to B.C.?" the officer asks, looking again inside the van.

I wave and smile. The officer turns to Rayne. "You'd better slow it down. I'm going to ask you to get back in the car and wait. I need to run this license through the system."

He reappears at the window looking much more stern. "Mr. Carpenter, you've had a few minor brushes with the law but nothing recent or outstanding. I hope that means you're cleaning up your act."

"Yes, Sir."

"I've had to write you up a ticket after all. I might have let you off, but you need to know that there are perks that come with having a clean slate. You, Sir, do not qualify for such favors."

He turns to Audrey and me.

"Now then, ladies…I'm going to need some identification from you as well, please."

Audrey reaches around in front of her seat. "Oh, good grief! My purse is gone. I don't have proof of anything anymore!"

"I need to see something, Ma'am. Do you have a driver's license, birth certificate, passport?" He turns to me and adds, "You too, Ma'am."

"A boy knocked me down and took my purse. I had everything in there," Audrey says.

The officer looks skeptical. "Did you report it?"

"No."

"Mine was stolen too," I say before he has a chance to ask Audrey any more questions.

"Is that a fact? Is that your backpack beside you?"

My face is getting very hot. "Oh, yes. I guess it is."

He nods toward the pack, the brim of his hat almost covering his face as he leans in. "Could you have a look in it, Ma'am, and tell me if there's any I.D. in there?"

I unzip the main pocket and swipe my hand around inside. "Nope, sorry. Nothing."

The officer looks up and down the road. "I'll have to ask you to come to the station with me then." He watches Rayne's face carefully. "These two ladies match the description of a missing person's report filed in Ottawa. Do you know anything about that?"

The color drains away from Rayne's neck. "I have nothing to do with that, Officer. If they're missing, I don't know anything about it."

"Didn't you say they were your grandmother and aunt? We need to identify them and sort out this situation. I'm asking you to follow me to the station. Remember, I know who you are." He looks at Audrey and me. "You can come with me in the cruiser."

He starts back toward his vehicle.

"Are we going in the police car?" Audrey asks.

"Jeezus, Audrey. You two better get your act together," Rayne says. "You need to make sure that if they identify you—and they probably have photos—I don't get blamed for kidnapping you or something. I'm innocent. All I've done is drive you around like you asked."

"Don't worry," I say. "By the way, nice to see how concerned you are for your granny and auntie when things get rough."

The ride to the station is sort of fun. I've never been in a police car before. Audrey talks the whole way.

"Are the sirens on? I can't hear them. Lillian, can you hear them? What are they going to do with us? We're not going to jail, are we? Young man, are we being arrested?"

"No. I'm just taking you in for questioning, Ma'am. I'm just concerned for your safety. To be honest, I'm a little worried about your collaboration with Mr. Carpenter."

"Rayne didn't do anything," Audrey says. "He's just driving us on our vacation."

The officer parks in a lot with several other police cruisers and opens the door for us. "Follow me."

Rayne looks like he is ready to run. I grab his hand and walk with him. "Don't worry," I say. "What's the worst that can happen?"

Inside, the officer speaks to a man at the desk and then puts Audrey and me in a room by ourselves. A lady officer comes in and closes the door.

"Hello, I'm Staff Sergeant Christensen." She shakes our hands. "And who are you?"

Audrey answers right away. "Lucy and Ethel."

"Lucy? Is that you?" she says to Audrey.

"No, I'm Ethel."

"Hmmm…because the officer mentioned that you called this lady Lillian."

"I did?" Audrey says. "Sometimes I forget."

"You forget your sister's name?"

"No. I have other sisters named Lillian."

Sergeant Christensen looks at me. "Lillian? Do you have identification?"

I shake my head and keep my eye on the backpack at my feet.

"Listen. Here's why we asked you to come in for questioning. We have two missing person's reports on file that match your descriptions and we need to investigate the possibility that you are these two. Now, if your name is Lillian," she says, "then you must be Lillian Gorsen, from Ottawa. Is that right, Lillian?"

"I'm Lucy, Lucy Smith." I can't really think of a good name under pressure.

"Audrey?" she says, turning.

"Yes?"

"So, you are Audrey? Audrey Clark?" Sergeant Christensen asks.

"Oh."

"Can you tell me why you are in Manitoba and why you left—" she checks her file, "Tranquil Meadows Nursing Home?"

We're caught. We are definitely in big trouble. "It was my idea," I say. "I just wanted to go on a vacation. It's boring in there. It's freezing and it's mashed potatoes and soggy toast the same, same, same every day. We got out on our own. That shows that we're capable of doing things. It's not easy to break out of there, you know; it's like a high-security prison with alarms in the elevators and codes for the doors."

"Where's Rayne?" Audrey asks.

"You mean Wayne," the officer says.

"No, Rayne."

"The man you came in with is Wayne Carpenter. He isn't your son, is he?"

"I like to think of him as my son," Audrey says. "But, who's Wayne? Did I hear wrong?"

"How did you meet Mr. Carpenter? Does he work at the nursing home?"

"No," I say. "We must have met him after."

"At the bank," Audrey says.

The officer's eyebrows pop like window blinds slipped from someone's grasp. "He met you at the bank?"

"Well, actually, in front of the bank. He helped us. We needed someone to drive." Audrey cups her hand beside her mouth and whispers that I'm not a very good driver.

"He had nothing to do with us leaving The Home," I say. "That's right. We met him after, and we asked him to drive us. It wasn't his idea, was it, Audrey? No, I'm sure it wasn't his idea."

Eventually, we convince Sergeant Christensen that we aren't being kidnapped or held for ransom or anything untoward. Audrey says, once again, how much she adores Rayne and wants him to be her son. She says that we sing and have picnics and that he drives safely most of the time. Sergeant Christensen leaves us alone in the room again. She returns with Rayne.

"First of all, Mrs. Clark, Mrs. Gorsen, we have verified that you are the women who have been reported missing, and I think you should know that your families and the administration at the nursing home have been worried sick about you." She turns to Rayne. "And you, Mr. Carpenter, have a less-than-stellar record and a history of rather poor judgment. I wonder if these ladies know that you have skirted around the edge of the law since you were a young teen?"

"I have no charges against me now," Rayne says. "There's nothing in my file that hasn't been resolved."

"True. Still, I think they should be aware that you are no innocent schoolboy."

"What happens now?" Rayne asks.

"I encourage you to return these two ladies to Ottawa and the safety of their home."

"Encourage?" Rayne says. "Are you saying they don't have to go home?"

Sergeant Christensen sighs. "Unfortunately, it isn't a crime to be missing. Adults can choose to leave home and cut off all contact with friends and family, and we can't do anything about it. But I have to stress that you are taking a risk. According to the report, Mrs. Gorsen and Mrs. Clark have Alzheimer's disease and can't always depend on their own judgment. I can see evidence of slight confusion, but it almost seems deliberate. I'm afraid that at this time, I don't deem them to be in danger, so I have to let you go." She turns to us. "I would like to have your permission to contact the nursing home and tell them that you're here and that you're safe."

I can't believe what I'm hearing. "You need our permission? We get to say whether or not you tell them?"

"That's the law. I can't divulge anything without your permission because you're adults. But the fact that they've filed a report tells me that they are very concerned. Why don't you call them from here to tell them yourselves?"

This is news to me. I thought that if we were caught, we would have to go back. This is great! We can just carry on if we want to—but, what about Albert? I should at least talk to him. He deserves to know where I am. Then again, he hasn't called or come looking for me, so why should I care? He's probably found some young thing at the office or maybe one of the uniforms to take my place. I pick up my bag and start for the door. To hell with him. "You can go ahead and call if you want, but just tell them that we're fine. Don't tell them where we are. I know Carol. She'll come right out here and get me, as long as it doesn't interfere with her work schedule. Yep, she'll come just to prove that she can. You can tell them we're having a grand old time and that we'll go back when we're good and ready."

"Audrey? Would you like to call someone?" the officer asks.

"No. I want to see the mountains and sit on a lawn chair with my bare feet in the ocean. I'll call them later too, when Lillian does."

Rayne grins. "See what I have to deal with? And you thought I was the difficult one."

Shadow is glad to see us. She crawls right up on my knee and snuggles in, her weight grounding me, clearing my head.

"You must have done a good job convincing them you were sane in there," Rayne says. "I have to admit, I was afraid I was goin' down. But the adventure continues. Way to go!"

"Can we still call you Rayne?" I ask. "I knew a boy in school named Wayne. I never really liked him."

"Call me Rayne. That's my name."

"That officer was so darned cute in that big hat," Audrey says.

"What exactly do you mean about convincing them we're sane?" I ask. "Do you think we're insane?"

"No, of course not. You know what I mean."

"I wish I'd been keeping a journal," Audrey says. "We have so many fun things to tell everyone when we get back."

There is a large stain on my mint-green pants. It looks like a distorted cartoon figure—big misshaped head and small body with arms and legs sprouting raggedly out, a brown splotch on my upper leg. I must have spilled tea or coffee there. Funny I haven't noticed until now. I look more closely at the rest of the clothes I'm wearing, surprised to see a paw print on my other leg and dirt on my sleeve. "Good grief," I say. "I'm a mess. Why didn't someone tell me I look like a street urchin? I need to do laundry."

No one answers. I reach for Shadow's foot, careful not to squeeze too tightly. She licks my hand. My thoughts bounce around like the balls inside a bingo cage, randomly dropping. Where are we going in this van and will we ever arrive? The landscape is unfamiliar and unexceptional. My clothes are filthy and so are my hands. Fraise seems to be sleeping. Luckily the driver looks awake and alert. My teacher will be wondering where I am. It has been days since I attended school, and my friend Charlotte will have no one to walk home with. I'm glad Blondie came along for the ride.

I look at my feet. I love these shoes with their bright colors, the white no longer perfectly white but beautiful nonetheless. They remind me of someone but who? I dig deep. Carol. Does Carol have shoes like these?

Outside, an ocean of brilliant golden-yellow blooms stretches north across a field. It takes my breath away. "What is that?"

"Sunflowers," the man answers.

"A field of sunflowers? People grow them like on a farm?"

"Yeah. They sell the seeds for oil and birdseed and roasted snacks."

"Can we stop and pick one?" I ask.

He checks the rearview mirror and turns abruptly off the highway at an exit just past the field. The lane leading to the farm is only a short way down the road. The man turns in, stops near the barn, and hops out. "Wait here," he says, and disappears into the barn. He returns with two stalks the breadth of his thumb, each supporting a mammoth sun-flower, and hands them to us. "To celebrate four days on the road." He smiles.

I reach out to take the flower. The stem has been tucked inside a brown paper bag that is crumpled up tightly around it to cushion the grip. I'm surprised to see the stem is hairy and rough. I'd not thought of it that way. I hold the stem in my lap, the bloom inches from my face. It has only an earthy scent, like the soil. I breathe it in and close my eyes. "Thank you," I tell the man. "Thank you for stopping."

We drive a short distance down the little road and park along the side to let the dog run.

Farther along the highway, signs point to Brandon.

"Is it time to stop?" Audrey asks. "I feel like we've been in this van for about a week without a break."

"It's almost three-thirty," the driver says. "We could stop, or we could drive another hour or so, cross into Saskatchewan, and stay somewhere just past that border."

"Saskatchewan already? Wow!" Audrey's vote is cast.

"That's fine," I say. I speak quietly to Shadow. "My back is killing me, but another hour or two isn't gonna make a difference, right Girl?" I still clutch the sunflower in my hand as it lies across my lap. I touch the petals, soft and layered; examine the center where the pointed tips of seeds form an intricate pattern of black, changing to dark brown nearer the rim of the circle. Things are so different when you look more closely at them.

14

I SWING MY ARM over the back of the seat and grope around for the bananas. They're cradled in a nook between the soft straps of a backpack.

"Anyone want a banana?" I ask, snapping off two and passing them to the front. I eat one. It's just right—not too hard or too ripe. I peel another; notice the firm sweetness and the way it comforts as it slides down my throat.

"Where are we going?" I ask.

"Saskatchewan."

"Is that where Sasquatch lives?"

"No, that's farther west, on the coast," Rayne says.

"It sounds like he should live in Saskatchewan, don't you think?"

"What about Albert?" Audrey asks. "Does Albert live in Alberta?"

"No. I don't think so."

A great expanse meanders on either side of the van without so much as a ripple or dip. We are a small speck. So much space is disconcerting. At home it's crowded but I don't mind. I share a bedroom with my sisters, and space at the table is always cramped. My brothers take up more room than they should with sharp elbows and big feet. Eleanor too, with her bursts of Italian and waving of arms.

The horizon is so far away. "Where are we going?"

"Saskatchewan," Rayne answers.

We cross into Saskatchewan and stop for a washroom break at the visitor information center. Audrey picks up pamphlets to look at and reads them aloud as we drive until she starts to feel nauseated.

"I guess I shouldn't read in the car," she says.

"You're a good reader," I say. "I love when people read to me. It's smooth on my head. Don't you love it, Rayne, when people read to you?"

"I wouldn't know."

"Your mom didn't read to you when you were little?"

He doesn't answer.

"I bet she did. *House at Pooh Corner* or *Treasure Island* or *Tom Sawyer*? Those are great books."

"Yeah. And right after she finished reading to me, we went outside and watched unicorns jump over rainbows. It was one big hug-fest at the Carpenter house."

"What do you mean?" Audrey asks.

"She left when I was ten."

"Oh, I'm so sorry."

"Yeah, me too. I came home from school one day and she was gone. Dad was there, crying—clumsy, slobbering, pissed out of his mind. I went upstairs and sat in her room until it got dark. I could smell her—the patchouli and the cream she always put on her face after she washed. All her clothes and things were still there, so I thought she'd come back but she never did. I puked every morning after that because I didn't want to go to school. I was afraid she'd come home and I wouldn't be there."

Rayne is so sad now, and it's my fault. "Not everyone has a mom that reads. I wish I hadn't said that."

"Forget it."

"Why did she leave?" Audrey asks.

"Do we really have to talk about this?"

"Yes," Audrey says. "We should talk about it. Friends should talk about these sorts of the things."

"She'd always spent a lot of time in her room, just lying there, and she wouldn't talk for days. What did I know? I was ten. I thought moms acted that way. I didn't know she had a lot of stuff goin' on in her head that she couldn't deal with. I realized as I got older, that she was clinically depressed. She and Dad used to fight a lot, but Dad would always give in when it got loud and dirty. I guess he was trying to protect me."

Audrey's gaze is fixed on Rayne's face. We drive in silence, none of us knowing what else to say. Until now, I knew nothing about this young man. I didn't even think of him as having a history, of being a child, even though I struggle with people who only see me only as nothing more than an old lady with dementia. It always makes me angry.

"Do you hear from her?" Audrey asks.

"Not once. Gran used to get in touch with her somehow, and that's the only way we'd know she was still alive. I guess she was in and out of hospitals a lot."

"That's so sad!" Audrey says. "You poor kid. I'm going to adopt you."

"What about your dad?" I ask.

"He tried, but we didn't always get along. I guess we were both dealing with the fallout in our own way. He's a good guy. He made sure I had clothes and food and everything, he just wasn't very good at knowing when I needed more, like when I needed someone to read to me." He glances at me in the rearview mirror. "Thank God my grandma lived just down the street. I spent a lot of time with her. She got me through it."

Audrey's face brightens. "That's why you came back to help us. You said we remind you of your grandma, right?"

"Yeah, but why I came back is still up for debate. I also know what it feels like to have a mom leave and not know where she's gone. You're not gonna want to hear this, Lillian, but even though your kids are adults now, it's still gotta be tough on them. For me, that's hard to reconcile."

"Oh, dear." I suddenly feel wretched. Too much bad news. My stomach reels and my mouth tastes like that salty spray the dental assistant blasts on my teeth when she's supposed to be cleaning them.

"Pull over. Pull over. I'm gonna be sick. Jeez Louise, pull over!" I scream.

Rayne slows and swerves onto the shoulder. He opens my door just in time and stands back. My stomach turns inside out.

Rayne hands me a paper towel to wipe my face and pours me a glass of water from the jug in the back. "I think we'd better stop in the next town," he says.

We pull off the highway at the next exit. "Welcome to Moosomin, population twenty-five hundred," he says.

There are a couple of hotels on the way into town and another just off the main street. "I think we should probably stay in one on the outskirts," Rayne says.

"You're afraid we're gonna wander off." I say.

"No, because you're not going anywhere without telling me, right?"

"Yes," Audrey says.

"Yes," I say. "But I want to stay in town. It would be nice to walk to supper and feel like we're free and not held hostile."

"Hostage?" Rayne says. "You feel like you're being held hostage?"

I don't answer.

"You're free to go if that's how you feel. I'm only trying to help."

Still, I don't answer. I know Rayne is angry but so am I. Why is he trying to control us? Isn't that what Audrey and I were trying to escape from? "You're our driver, not our babysitter," I say, my face drawn in a stern frown.

Audrey looks back at me in surprise. "That's not right. Rayne's more than just our driver, Lillian."

"Of course he's more to you; he's your boyfriend. I'm sick of both of you."

"Okay," Rayne says calmly. "That's enough. Everyone needs to chill. I'll find a motel and we'll all rest."

"Right," I say. "You plan it, and we'll just do whatever you say. Is that what you want?"

"Fine. What do you want to do?" Rayne asks as he continues to drive toward the edge of town.

"I told you I want to stay in town."

I look at the sunflower hastily thrown to the floor when I vomited. The petals are wilted and the bloom itself is leaning to the side like a doll's head, too heavy for the worn neck that used to support it.

We pull into a driveway to turn around and head back into town. No one says a word.

Parked in front of a motel half a block from Main Street, Rayne turns off the engine. "Do you want to go in and register? I'll wait here."

I'm suddenly unsure of how to do this. It all seems new and complicated. Even our names are not ours to claim now, and I can't recall what name I'm supposed to use. I reach for Shadow and scratch her head.

"Let's all go in," Audrey says. "It'll be fine."

"Do you want to be Ethel and Lucy, my grandma and aunt again?" Rayne asks. "Lillian, what do you want to do?"

I continue to pet Shadow, refusing to look up. "I want to wait here. You two go in and I'll stay with Shadow."

"You sure?" Rayne asks.

I nod and avoid making eye contact.

Rayne stuffs the keys in his pocket and walks to the other side to help Audrey out. Even with his help and her cane, she struggles to walk to the door, stiff from so much time in the car, bent forward like she is running a race, only slow and halting. I don't remember her looking so old.

I read and re-read the sign outside the motel. *Moosomin Inn, your home away from home.* Rayne's words echo in my ears. Are my kids worrying and wondering where I am? A lump rises in my throat and I swallow hard. Tom and Carol are grown and accustomed to living their own lives. They aren't ten. Surely I can't be accused of abandoning them. My clenched fists loosen slightly. I read the sign again—*your home away from home.* It is comforting somehow, like a greeting card that tells you the thing you want to hear.

Rayne and Audrey return to the car and we park outside the room. The throbbing ache in my back sends pain stabbing down into my leg.

"Oh, my," I groan, easing onto my feet with the help of the doorframe. Shadow bounds past me and into Rayne's grasp.

"Oh no you don't," he says, snapping the leash onto her collar.

Rayne carries our bags in and sets them on the beds. No one talks. I've said something wrong, something to cause this chill. I must have. Rayne turns to leave.

"I'm glad you're here," I say.

"No problem," Rayne says on the way out the door. He disappears into the room next door.

I examine the hands of the clock on the wall. "Is it eight-thirty?" I ask.

Audrey looks at the digital clock on the bedside table. "Five-eighteen."

I look back at the clock on the wall. "No, it says eight-thirty. No, nine o'clock."

"Five-eighteen," Audrey says again.

"Why is that extra hand on the clock? It goes around and around so fast and makes it hard to tell what time it is."

"I know. I have trouble with that too," Audrey says. "This kind is much clearer." She taps the bedside clock, drawing my attention there.

"You're right," I say. "Five-nineteen." I move the pack from my bed and lie flat on my back, and close my eyes.

It is very dark when I wake. Audrey is lying motionless in the next bed, so I pull the blankets up and stare at the ceiling. Here we are—God knows where—heading to places unknown, and it's good, really good. I rise from bed and stumble about looking for my purse. In my notebook, I write the names of my friends. These, I remember without a problem:

Audrey. Rayne. Shadow.

A couple of other things pop into my head and I write them down too:

sunflowers. tired.

I check the clock. Twelve thirty-seven. I lie back down and shut my eyes. The wind howls outside, and the vent in the ceiling pops like those plastic packing bubbles when you squeeze them. Audrey wheezes and snorts.

The day dawns calm and bright. I sit on the side of the bathtub, pull on the tap, and dangle my fingers in the running water, waiting for it to warm up. I pull and turn, push the tap and wait. Still, it runs cold. Finally, I turn it off and wash up at the sink.

There is a knock at the bathroom door. "Can I come in? I need to go."

Audrey rushes in.

"Just finished. It's all yours," I say. "Just don't try to have a bath. The water's freezing."

We meet up with Rayne and find a small diner a block away.

"I called my dad last night," Rayne says. "He actually

sounded happy to hear from me. We had the usual awkward silences where he tries not to say what he's really thinking and I try not to notice, but I think it's gonna be okay."

The waitress brings the food.

"Did you tell him about us?" Audrey asks.

"Not specifically. I told him I'm traveling with friends."

Audrey's smile is huge. "We heard you playing your guitar this morning. You're very talented."

I'm pretty sure he's blushing.

"We'll be in Regina by noon and then Swift Current or maybe even the Alberta border by late afternoon. We'll see how the day goes," Rayne says. "What do you think about that, Lillian?"

"Sounds good. Are we really almost to Alberta? That's where the Rocky Mountains start I think. I've never been in the mountains before."

"You're gonna love it. We don't get into serious elevations until we get to Calgary and west of there, but we'll be into the foothills before that."

"I like it here. Do we have to go somewhere today? It would be nice just to rest and maybe shop or something," Audrey says.

"I think we should keep going," Rayne says. "It's day five and people must be getting anxious to hear from you."

"What people?" I ask.

"Nursing home people and your families," Rayne answers. "I wonder what they said when the police called to tell them you're safe. We should have stuck around to find out. The police weren't supposed to say where you were, but it wouldn't be hard to find out where the call originated."

"We should keep moving," I say. "Besides, I'm anxious to see the mountains."

Audrey scoops the last of the scrambled eggs into her mouth and washes them down with coffee. There is a bright red smudge of ketchup on her sleeve but she doesn't seem to notice.

15

ON OUR WAY OUT of town, I pull my pen and paper out. The colors outside are as vivid as acrylic paint in the midmorning sun. I imagine myself walking to the horizon in my navy pants and pale blue shirt; picture the trek as color wading through color.

To my right, Shadow too, is watching the scenery fly by, her nose mashed against the window trailing smudge marks as she turns and jostles with the motion of the van. She is fascinated, standing on the seat and taking it all in. She pants, her tail wags then stops, then wags again. She whimpers, then she's silent. What does she see? What does she think? Does she understand that the world out there is separate from the world in the van?

I run my hand down Shadow's back. She turns and licks me and tries to inch up onto my knee, settling for a precarious balancing act, back legs on the floor and front paws in my lap, gazing at me eye-to-eye. I laugh and throw my arms around her neck.

We've been driving forever. My backside is sore but I'm not complaining. We have a purpose now—to get farther away and to see the mountains.

"Look at that," Rayne says, pointing across the plains at two grain elevators, one nearby and one in the distance.

"It looks like a postcard," I say.

"They're tearing them down—the grain elevators. I don't know much about how they grow and store grain now, but I understand hundreds of the old wooden elevators have been demolished. It seems wrong. It just feels like they need to be there standing guard over the fields and towns."

"You hold on pretty tightly to tradition for a young guy," Audrey says, looking at his profile as he drives. "You love old things, admit it."

"Old things, not necessarily old people," he says.

"Hey! I know you don't mean that."

"You think I'm joking?" Rayne looks at Audrey and smiles.

"No need to share this with anyone, right?" he says. "I don't want it getting around that I'm all sensitive and empathetic."

"Secrets are safe with us," I say.

"Yeah," Rayne says. "Sorry."

"Where are we now?" I ask.

"Outside of Regina."

"Almost to the mountains?" asks Audrey.

"Tomorrow we'll start to see mountains," Rayne says.

"Let's keep going so we can make that happen."

"Where do you live, Audrey?" I ask, leaning forward as far as my seatbelt will allow.

"Ottawa. I've always lived there."

"I know, but where? Do you have a house?"

"Yep," Audrey says. "Terry and I live in a house on Griffin Avenue." She pauses. "No—we used to but Terry died."

"Do you still live there?"

"I think so."

"Do I live there too?" I ask.

"Yes, we all do. Not you," Audrey says, pointing at Rayne. "A lot of people live there and we have a big dining room where we all eat."

She's right. I remember the room now. "And that lady sits at our table."

"Yeah."

The fields of wheat are separated by rows of trees. I imagine that from a plane they must look like a quilt, the patchwork stitched together in straight, dark lines. I catch sight of a road sign pointing south of the highway. "*Welcome to Moose Jaw, the Friendly City,*" I read aloud.

"The friendly city. We should go there."

Rayne agrees. "Why not? We could use a break. Let's take half an hour to see what Moose Jaw is all about."

We drive into the city.

"A casino!" Audrey says. "Can we go there?"

Rayne laughs. "Really?"

"Yeah. It'll be a new experiment for me. Have you ever been to a casino, Lillian?"

"Never. Let's do it," I say.

"We don't have much cash to spare," Rayne warns.

"How much do we need?"

He pulls into the parking lot. "Twenty dollars each could last two minutes or two hours. Depends on whether you're lucky or not."

Audrey is already out of her seatbelt and opening the door. "Come on Lillian, this is gonna be fun."

The lobby has high ceilings and a muffled, velvety feel underfoot. A man in a suit smiles and nods, then speaks to Rayne.

He examines Rayne's driver's license, then quickly thanks him and welcomes him through.

"What was that about?" I ask.

"Just wanted to make sure I was over eighteen."

"Good heavens," I say. "That's odd. I wonder why he doesn't ask us."

The lobby opens up into a much larger room filled with color and flashing lights, beeping, and ringing bells. Machines line every wall and fill every space with bright scrolling numbers and images. In the middle of the room, people in shirts and ties stand at tables, spinning wheels and dealing cards.

"What do we do?" Audrey shouts.

"Follow me." Rayne leads us past the gaming tables and several machines that wink and whir. He stops in front of a bank of slot machines that all display the same three images in different orders: big red number sevens, sevens engulfed in flames, and black rectangles with the word *bar* emblazoned on them.

"Blazing Sevens is the easiest to understand," Rayne says, "You bet three quarters at a time."

We find two unoccupied machines beside each other and squeeze into the seats. Rayne stands behind.

"Now, take a twenty-dollar bill and feed it into the slot," he says.

We do as we're told and the display shows eighty credits.

"Always bet the full amount on each roll," he says. He reaches over Audrey's shoulder and points to the *max bet* button. "Push that."

Audrey touches the button and looks up at the screen. A burning seven, a regular seven and a bar line up along the line.

"Did I win anything?" she asks.

"Nope. Try again," Rayne says. He shows her how to hit the *single bet* button three times and pull the handle. She likes that.

"This is what I imagined it would be like," she says, her face wrinkling into a huge smile.

I watch carefully. "I don't get it," I say. "How do you win?"

Rayne points to the line that runs across the center of the screen. "Any time three matching icons land on the line, you win. If it's three bars or three sets of three bars, you win ten or twenty or forty quarters. If it's three sevens, you win hundreds and three blazing sevens..." he points up at the video display above, "you win that...six hundred and seventy-two dollars."

"That's very complicated. Just watch me and tell me if I win." I push the *max bet* button. Three sevens show up in the display screen but not evenly aligned.

"I win. I got three sevens," I say, tapping Audrey on the arm.

"I'm afraid not," Rayne says. "They have to be on the line."

"Hell's bells! That's not fair." I stare at the screen, willing the numbers to move into synch. I pound my fist down on the button and one of each picture choice spreads unevenly across the screen. "I don't like this game. Let's go." I pick up my purse and stand up to leave.

"I'm not done yet," Audrey says. "Am I?" She looks at Rayne. "How do I know when I'm done?"

He points to the smaller number on the panel. "You have sixty-five credits left and Lillian has seventy-four."

On her next pull of the handle, Audrey spins three triple bars and her total goes up to one hundred and five. This is getting more interesting.

Audrey hoots with excitement and continues to play. In minutes, her twenty dollars are gone.

My machine still boasts seventy-four credits. I glare at the display screen, decide I'm ready to continue. I push the *single bet* three times slowly, deliberately, then reach up and pull the handle. One blazing seven, two blazing sevens, one double bar.

"Damn!" I slide awkwardly from my chair and step back. "This isn't as much fun as I thought. Can I get my money back?"

"You still have some credits. Do you want to cash out?" Rayne asks.

"Yes. I'm done," I say. I feel a pout forming on my lips.

Rayne reaches over to hit the *cash out* button but instead, hits *max bet*.

Three sevens, surrounded in flames, pop into place along

the center line. A bell rings out and a light on top of the machine spins, splashing red on Rayne's face.

"What on earth? Did we win?" Audrey's eyes grow wide.

"Oh, yeah!" Rayne says. "You two have an amazing lucky streak that follows you around."

Audrey raises her hands in the air and shouts. "Yahoo! The big one? Did we win the big one?"

He doesn't answer at first. He looks at the screen, lowers his voice and says, "No, not the big one. But we did win something."

A lady in a blue suit approaches with keys jangling from her hand. She slides the key into a slot and the flashing light and bells stop. "How would you like your winnings?" she asks, looking at Rayne.

"Cash, please," he says.

"I'll be right back." The woman leaves us standing in front of the machine, a bit disoriented and very pleased.

"It's that easy?" I ask. "She'll come back with cash and we get to leave?"

"Yep. It seems simple. It doesn't usually work that way when I gamble, but today we got lucky."

The man at the machine beside mine nods congratulations in our direction. I feel like a celebrity. Players at nearby terminals watch the attendant return with the money. She counts it out into Rayne's palm, but with all the confusion, I can't see or hear the amount. He tucks it into his pocket.

We follow Rayne out through the maze of machines and past the man in the lobby. Inside the van, Rayne hands each of us fifty dollars.

"Congratulations," he says.

"That's it?" I ask. "With all the lights and bells, it seemed like we won millions."

"Yeah, that's just to keep everyone playing; it adds to the excitement. You made money though, right? That's better than most people in there."

"I guess you're right," I say.

"Time's up. We need to get back on the road."

Audrey sits up straight, her shoulders back and head high. "That was fun! Did you see me get three bars? I won too."

Rayne glances over at her as he pulls out of the parking lot. "Yeah, we all won."

I stuff the bills in my purse and open my notebook: *sevens on fire. bright lights. winning at the casino.*

Audrey starts to sing, softly at first, her voice rising with each line.

"Oh, we ain't got a barrel of money,
Maybe we're ragged and funny,
But we travel along, singin' our song,
Side by side."

I join in and together, we finish the song, every word familiar, every note true.

"We sang that in the car, my mom and I," Audrey says. "Dad didn't sing. He just drove. We lived on the farm on the outskirts of Ottawa, near Blackburn. We'd go into town on Saturdays to shop for groceries and I'd get some licorice or gumballs. I felt like everything was fine when we sang, everything would be okay."

I reach over to pet Shadow. "Albert sings that song to me when I'm worried about money. There's always something we need, something that's broken and needs to be replaced—never enough money with little kids. He holds my hand and sings and we laugh."

I run my hand repeatedly, rhythmically down Shadow's back, smoothing and smoothing her hair.

"Terry always worries about the money. We live modestly, and with no kids we don't really need much. I squirrel away what I can for our retirement." Audrey looks like she isn't sure whether or not to go on. "Terry is...good to me. He worries about me a lot. He always says 'For God's sake, why didn't you call to say you were gonna be late?'" She stops and rubs her hands together as if she's cold.

"Why does he always want to know where you are?" I ask. "It would drive me crazy, having to report in all the time."

"No. He loves me. He doesn't like me talking to other men though. Sometimes I have to do fittings for men's suits, alterations for pants and things. He hates that—says it isn't right. Now, I let on that I just do women's alterations. It's just easier not to upset him. I never actually lie, I just don't tell him everything."

I nod. "I guess I'm lucky that way. Albert doesn't worry like that. I do a lot of things on my own and with friends. Nothing too daring mind you, but Albert's always good about it. He'll say 'You go ahead; the kids and I will handle it' and they do—better than me sometimes."

Audrey nestles more comfortably into her seat and hums quietly until she dozes off.

"I should have brought my knitting along for the trip," I say. "I could have finished that sweater for Carol if I'd known we'd be gone so long, the one with the kittens."

Albert tightens his grip on the steering wheel. "We'll be there before you know it."

"Is Fraise asleep up there?" I ask. "Honestly, she can fall asleep anywhere. I bet she could sleep standing up in the middle of traffic."

"She's tired," Albert says. "Why don't you have a nap too?"

"No, I'll keep you company. It's the least I can do; you're so good to me."

I turn my attention to the dog. "Blondie, come here, Puppy."

She raises her head and wags her tail but remains curled up on the floor.

"Good girl, stay," I say. I hold my hands out and look closely at my wedding band. I spin it around on my finger so it sits perfectly positioned there. "My ring is getting too big, I should have it resized. I must be getting thinner."

Fraise's rumbling breath draws my attention back to the front seat.

"It's funny that Fraise never married, don't you think? Thank goodness she didn't though. If she was busy with her own family, she might not have been so attentive to us when we were kids. I'm so glad we're back together again. I kind of let her slip out of my life a bit when I got busy with the kids and teaching and everything. Why do we do that? Why do we let the people we love just fade into the background like that?"

"You know what? This would be a great time for you to relax and have a sleep," Albert says, a little too persuasively. "We still have a ways to go before we stop, so just put your head back and rest."

I breathe deeply and shut my eyes. My head is pounding.

When had that started? The pain is centered just over my eyebrows, like a heavy rubber band pulled too tightly. Beneath the band, the pain seeps down behind my eyes. I rub my temples, circling my fingertips round and round and press in.

The hum of tires against the road soothes the pain a bit and the vibration massages my neck. I recline in my seat, eyes closed, listening.

Albert's breathing is slow and deep—always steady as a rock, that man—my foundation. Tom is a noisy breather. He doesn't really snore as much as he purrs. The air sort of sputters around in his throat on its way in and out, as if it's feeding a tiny outboard motor. Carol's breath is shallow and quick, like she's in a hurry even in her sleep. That's Carol all right—busy, busy, busy—too busy to breathe deeply. Too busy to stay at home, eat dinner with us, spend time. I can't complain though. Here we all are, together, heading somewhere with Albert at the helm.

"Albert, what about my job? I can't just leave the students behind with no teacher. Take Daniel—no one understands him like I do. He doesn't get math unless I present it in hockey terms—you know—if your team is second in the standings and the first-place team is 8-0 and 3 and your team has won 6 games, what is the score? That sort of thing. He can figure it out in a flash as long as it involves hockey. And Jean needs to sit near the front. She can't concentrate at the back. And Sarah—if she says she has to go to the bathroom, she means it. The students need me.

"There is always marking to be done, too. I should have brought it along. But it is summer. Of course—summer holidays—that's why we're all together. We must be going camping." My muscles relax and I imagine the scent of pine as we zip ourselves into the tent.

16

HIGHWAY 628 NORTH EAST, *Waldeck Access Road; Central Waldeck Access Road; West Waldeck Access Road; Airport Road to Swift Current Airport.* I'm reading the signs along the highway. Rayne and Audrey are very quiet, their eyes focused straight ahead along the white line that leads to who-knows-where.

"Where's Swift Current?" I ask.

"Saskatchewan," Rayne answers. "You're awake! How're you feeling?"

"I'm fine, a little groggy. Was I sleeping long?"

Rayne nods. "About an hour and a half. Gambling must have tired you out."

I'm not sure what he means. I wouldn't even know how to gamble. "Are we gonna stop soon?" I ask.

"Can you last a couple more hours?"

"I'll be okay with that as long as we have a quick bathroom break," Audrey says.

"Yeah, yeah, that's fine," I agree. I'm still tired. Maybe I'm hungry. What can I make for supper for the three of us?

"Could we get some potatoes and carrots and onions?" I ask. "I think I'll make a pot of stew for supper. I guess I'll need some meat too."

"Ooh, that sounds good," Audrey says.

"Where will you cook this stew?" Rayne asks. "Do you have a stove back there that I don't know about?"

I look around. "No, I guess not." We're in a van. Of course there's no stove. What was he thinking?

His tone is apologetic. "We'll look for a restaurant that serves home-cooked meals. Maybe they'll have stew on the menu."

"I just thought it would be something for me to do. I feel useless."

"It's your job to keep us entertained," Rayne says. "Tell us a joke."

"Hmmm. I'm terrible at telling jokes. I can never remember the punch line or the beginning or the middle." I smile at my own shortfall.

"Well, that makes it more difficult," Rayne says. "Audrey, know any jokes?"

"What's black-and-white and red all over?" Audrey asks.

"A newspaper—read all over?" Rayne says.

"No."

"A sunburned zebra?" I say.

"No."

"A nun rolling down a hill over shards of broken glass?" Rayne says.

"Oooh! No."

"What then?"

Audrey turns to look out the window. A minute later she asks, "Are we going to stop for that bathroom break?"

"What? You didn't tell us the answer to your joke," Rayne says.

"I don't remember the answer."

Rayne laughs, slowly at first. But he can't stop. He laughs until tears well in his eyes. He wipes them dry with his sleeve and drives on in silence.

We stop near Gull Lake at a roadside rest area, use the bathroom, and let Shadow out for a stretch, all without uttering a word.

Back on the highway, Audrey turns to Rayne. "I guess it was pretty funny that I couldn't remember the answer to that joke."

"No," Rayne says. "I wasn't laughing at you. It's just that I can't get a handle on this thing. You remember some things in such detail—things your husband said to you thirty years ago—and yet you forget halfway through a joke that you started thirty seconds ago. It doesn't make sense. It's crazy."

Audrey just looks at him with a blank stare.

"I'm sorry," he says.

"No offense taken, Dear. Here's one. What's the best thing about having Alzheimer's?"

"I don't know. What?"

"You don't remember that you don't remember. Did I say that right? Someone told me that and for some reason, it's the only joke I can remember."

I watch the plains slip past the window. Fences shape corrals and separate fields of horses from cattle. Grain grows in the spaces between.

"So much land," I say, marveling at the farms spread out on either side, barns and outbuildings outnumbering homes.

"It's a different lifestyle here," Rayne says. "Kids ride horses as soon as they can reach the stirrups."

"I've never ridden a horse," I say. "You must feel so alive up there, no seatbelt, no windshield, no roof."

"Sounds dangerous," Audrey says.

"But hairy and free."

I want to live on a ranch, care for horses, and ride as far as I can see without leaving my own property. I picture myself galloping through the fields and I fight the urge to cry. What if I never get to ride a horse? I am probably too old now, and as much as I hate to admit it, possibly too frail. Such a cruel way to finish out a life. It should be like reading a book—fine to have a sad part in the middle, but the ending should be happy.

The light is changing. It isn't dusk yet, but even through the tinted windows, I can see the touch of yellow-pink in the sky.

We pass into Alberta. A short distance down the road, there is a small stand of trees clustered together at the side of the highway—a tiny forest—a picture-perfect backdrop for a motel and adjoining diner.

Rayne slows and steers into the lot. "How's this look?"

"I'm so stiff and tired, a mattress tossed on the ground would look good to me," Audrey says.

"I'll take that as a yes then?"

"Yes for me too," I say, as I search for the release button on the seatbelt.

Inside the office, each of us massages a different body part—arm, shoulder, hip—while we wait in front of the desk.

Finally, a young girl appears from somewhere in the back. She strolls in and, without eye contact or greeting, steps behind the computer and prepares to type. "Name?" she says, barely looking up.

"Do you have two rooms for tonight?" Rayne asks.

"Yep. Name?"

"Rayne Carpenter."

"And?"

"Lucy and Ethel Jones," Audrey says, stepping forward as she speaks. "We're sisters."

The girl looks up briefly without expression and enters the names on the screen. We finish registering and, keys in hand, find our rooms.

"She was pretty rude," I say. "How old do you think she was? Not old enough to be running a motel, surely."

"Probably a high-school student," Rayne says. "Summer job, bored to death, pissed about having to work out here in the middle of nowhere. Or her parents own the place and expect her to work whenever she's not in school."

"Either way, it wouldn't kill her to crack a smile."

The rooms are clean and bright with big windows at the back overlooking the small woodlot. We open the window, and through the trees, I'm surprised to see that the ground slopes down to a river that bubbles and swirls past the motel, then swings away across the fields. I hadn't even seen the water from the highway.

Rayne and Shadow appear at the door.

"Want to go for a walk before supper?"

"You go ahead, Dear. I'm going to freshen up and when you get back, we'll eat," I say.

"I'll come with you," Audrey says to Rayne.

I start toward the bathroom. "We haven't eaten yet, have we?"

Rayne looks at me, the corners of his mouth creasing downward. I know that expression, that look that means I've said something crazy.

"I'll be fine. I can manage on my own for five minutes. Go ahead. Jeez Louise! I'm not a child."

I watch the three of them round the corner of the building before I turn to go into the bathroom. The full-length mirror inside forces me to stand up straighter. I examine my reflection, starting with the flashy shoes and moving up to the little bulge that swells under my shirt at the tummy, the rounded shoulders, gray hair, and sagging skin on my face.

"You look old, Girl, but not half bad. I'd have to say you look better now than you have for months."

The splash of warm water on my face is like a long, firm hug. The towel is plush and smells of fabric softener. I hold it on my face and breathe deeply. I love this place.

Voices in the other room tell me they're back.

"The smells coming from the diner are great," Audrey says. "Are you ready to eat?"

"I sure am."

The hiss of hot grease bubbling up from the baskets of home-cut fries and the scrape of large metal spatulas flipping hamburger patties on the steel grill draw me in. We sit near the back by the window. The late afternoon sun is still high enough in the sky to cast shadows on our table.

"We're getting closer," Rayne says. "By tomorrow we should start to see mountains in the distance."

"Did you ever think we'd get this far?" Audrey asks.

"A few times I didn't think we'd make it out of Ontario," Rayne says. "I still can't believe it, to be honest."

I shake my head. "I knew we would."

Rayne smiles. "You're pretty sure of most things."

"Except when I'm not…not sure of anything."

"I guess we could all say the same," Rayne says. "That's what keeps us humble."

I don't like talking about these things, what we did yesterday, what we'll do tomorrow. I only care about now, right now. I pick at my fries; stab one at a time and swallow before stabbing another.

"Maybe when we get there, I'll introduce you to my dad, and we could show you around," Rayne says. "I'm sure he'd say you could stay with us for a few days, but then we'll need to make arrangements for you to get back to Ottawa."

This catches me totally off guard.

"We should call your families from here, and they can book flights. They might want to fly out to join you for the trip back, or I can take you to the airport and they can meet you at the other end."

I put down my fork. I haven't thought about how we will get back until now. How could this have happened? I must have known Rayne would stay in B.C. Maybe I thought we would stay there too. No…. I really haven't even considered it.

"I don't think we should call yet. They don't see us like you do. They'd never trust us to finish the trip. They think we're helpless."

"I'll talk to them, convince them," Rayne says. He seems so confident.

Audrey has stopped eating and is listening. "They're gonna blame you for this. They think we're just clueless old ladies," she says.

I bury my face in my hands. "I've made such a mess of this."

What a selfish old woman I've become, only thinking of myself. A fog circles my head. I search in my purse for the room key, pull out some bills and put them on the table.

"I need to lie down. Please finish your meals. I'll be fine."

"I'll come with you," Rayne says, rising to his feet.

"Just stay here. I'm just going to lie down."

He sits back down, and I leave the diner. My legs are behaving. They're taking me in the right direction, I think, but my head is blurry. I walk past the first few rooms, peer through the windows. Nothing is familiar. Farther along, I recognize the van.

The curtain is open in the room nearest the van. I lean close to the window, shade my eyes, then jump back, nearly losing my balance. Shadow has seen me and leapt up to the window.

I try the key. The door opens and Shadow is there wagging her tail. I glance back toward the restaurant. Rayne is standing just outside, watching. He waves and steps back inside. I burrow into the room and lie on the bed with Shadow close beside.

I concentrate hard, trying to breathe deeply and evenly. I learned this from a few yoga classes I attended somewhere. It helps.

My father was always calm and composed, always

confident. He treated me as an adult even when I was young. He'd say 'You know the answer Lilly, just ask yourself and listen. The answer's there.' Sometimes I just wanted him to tell me the right thing to do but that wasn't his way. He trusted me. I wish I knew where he was so I could ask him now.

Albert is so much like my dad. I didn't see that before. Why is he not here with me? Where is he?

He's dead.

The thought comes to me like a recording, an announcement that's repeated several times through the day reminding me of rules that need to be observed or what time the next bus will arrive. It is informative. Just so I'll know.

Rayne is a child with an old soul. He watched me walk back to the room. He trusts me, but only so far. What would my own kids have done if I'd asked them to take me on this trip? If they weren't too busy?

Shadow scrambles to her feet as someone knocks at the door. I ease up and shuffle to open it. It's Rayne and Audrey.

"Sorry. You have the key," Audrey says.

"It's okay. I was awake."

They follow me into the room. We sit together at the small table, near the door. Rayne sets a Styrofoam container in front of me, along with a cardboard cup of coffee.

"You didn't finish. We thought you might be hungry."

"Thank you." I poke a couple of lukewarm fries into my mouth.

"Are you feeling better?" Audrey asks.

"Yeah, I think I am." I sip the coffee. It's hot and fresh. "We should call the kids, like you said."

Rayne looks at me from the corner of his eye. "Are you sure?"

I nod and take another sip.

"I think it's a good idea," he says. "They've already heard that you're okay, but if we call them, they'll be able to start planning your return. I'm glad you've changed your mind."

"Who should we call about me?" Audrey asks.

"We'll start with the nursing home and they can give us everyone else's numbers," Rayne says.

"Will you come back with us?" Audrey asks.

"No, I'm going to stay with my dad for awhile. I realized this week how much I miss him."

"You're not coming? When will we see you again?" Audrey asks with a devastated look on her face.

"I...I don't know," he says. "I'll definitely visit you next time I'm in Ottawa. You can count on that." He brightens. "But we still have things to see together. I can't wait to drive you through the mountains and all the way to the Pacific Ocean. It's gonna blow you away."

"What do you mean?"

"It's freakin' amazing. You're gonna love it."

I stuff another fry into my mouth and close the container. I try to swallow. There is a lump in my throat that wasn't there a minute ago. I notice a phone on the desk.

"How do we do this? Can we call from the room?"

"You can," Rayne says. "I bought a long-distance card the other day to call my dad. You can use it."

"I don't know the number."

"I can call it for you," he says, "and then you can explain."

He dials directory assistance, asks for the number, and jots it down on the motel paper. "Are you sure you want to do this?" he asks.

"I'm sure." My stomach reels.

Rayne keys in the nursing home number. "Hello. My name is Rayne. I'm calling on behalf of Lillian—" He pauses and whispers, "What's your last name again?"

"Lillian Gorsen and Audrey—Clark," he says after prompting Audrey as well.

"Hello, yes, they're fine. They're here. Lillian would like to talk to you."

He hands me the receiver.

"Hello?"

The voice on the other end answers cautiously, "Lillian, is that you?"

"Yes."

"Where are you?" I hear the woman whisper to someone else, "It's Lillian and Audrey. Shh."

"Where are we?" I ask, looking to Rayne for the answer. "We're in Alberta," I say. "We're fine."

"Alberta? How on earth did you get there?" the woman asks.

"We drove."

Silence.

"We drove in the van," I say.

"Is Audrey there?"

"Yes, she's right here. Do you want to talk to her?"

"No. No, that's okay. I believe you. How did you drive that far? How did you know the way?" The woman sounds flustered, not sure what to ask.

I'm not sure what else to say either. I hand the phone to Rayne and slump down in the closest chair.

"Hello," Rayne says again.

He listens.

"Yes, well, I drove most of the way—no, I'm just a friend." His brow wrinkles and his hand clenches tightly. "I only drove them because they asked me to at first. I didn't know they were running away. I just thought they were two ladies who were heading west on vacation. They invited me to go along because I live in B.C. and was looking for a way home."

He listens for another moment then turns white and starts to sweat. I take the phone back from him.

"Listen, Rayne is our friend. He helped us. He hasn't done anything wrong. Do you understand? We only called to let you know we're fine."

The woman on the phone pumps me with questions.

"Where exactly are you? Is there a number where we can get in touch with you? What were you thinking? Why haven't you called before now?"

Rayne reaches out his hand to take up the challenge again. I return the phone to him.

"Hello. Listen, Lillian and Audrey are doing fine. They want to see the Rockies, and we're almost there. We thought we should call you and their families to let them know, and to see what suggestions they might have for returning them to Ottawa. Do you have their relatives' phone numbers?"

His pen is poised, waiting.

"Hello—yes—Rayne. I explained it all to the other woman. We were hoping to get the phone numbers of Carol and Tom and someone for Audrey…. No, I don't know the number here."

Eventually, Rayne writes down three phone numbers, thanks the woman, and hangs up the phone.

"They wanted me to talk to the supervisor and to give

them the number here," he says. "But they did give me these." He holds up the notepad.

I am shaking. I try to remember why I agreed to do this. I feel like I'm back in school in Mr. Lacey's office, explaining that I haven't done anything wrong.

Rayne nudges me gently. "Do you want to call Carol first or Tom?"

"Maybe Tom first," I say, hoping for a less dramatic confrontation.

Rayne dials the number. He listens for a male voice and then hands me the receiver.

"Hello?" I say.

"Mom? Where the hell are you?"

I'm glad he formed the question this way. Somehow the brusqueness gives me the courage to go on. "Hello, Tom. How are you and the kids?"

"Where are you?"

"Alberta."

Just like the lady in the phone call before this, he is suddenly at a loss for words.

"Alberta? What the hell? How did you get there?"

"Look, Honey. I called to tell you I'm fine and that I've gone on a lovely vacation with my old friend, Audrey, and a new friend, Rayne."

"A vacation! Are you kidding? Why would you plan a vacation without telling anyone at Tranquil Meadows or without telling us?"

"I'm forgetful, not stupid. Let's just say I knew you wouldn't let me go. My plan did have a few flaws though. But then this young man helped us figure things out, and now we're in Alberta. You can't imagine how much fun I've had."

"Really? Who is this guy, this Ryan. What's his story?"

"Who?"

"Ryan, your new friend who helped you figure things out. Who is he?"

"Oh, Rayne. He's just a nice young man. Like you."

"You didn't give him your bank account number or your credit cards, did you?"

"I might have. I don't remember, but if I did, the money will still be there. Here, you can talk to him."

Rayne raises his eyebrows and wipes his hand across his forehead. He starts right in without waiting for Tom to speak.

"I know how this must sound," he says, "but believe me, I didn't realize your mom had run away when I agreed to drive her and Audrey to British Columbia. When I found out, a couple of days into the trip, I did a lot of soul-searching but this felt like the right thing to do. Your mom is a great lady and she's had a great time. It's all good, Man. I get that you're angry about not knowing where she was, but now you know. Now we need to figure out how to get her and Audrey back to Ottawa safely."

Rayne holds the receiver away from his ear and I can hear Tom's voice, loud and clear.

"Look, Asshole, I'm not as gullible as my mother. What's your angle? How much is this gonna cost us to get her back safely. Is there a ransom?"

"No, of course not. I don't want anything. Look, I might not have had the best intentions when this whole thing started, I'll admit that. But things have changed. I just want them to see the mountains and get safely back home."

"Put my mother on the phone."

He hands the phone back to me.

"You can't just trust people, Mom. Not everyone has your best interest in mind. You're an easy target."

"But he only did what we asked," I say.

"I'm going online right now to check your account."

I hear him tapping on the keyboard and then his voice. "Hmmm…. Looks like you took out money in Ottawa the first day. What's this thousand dollars you withdrew two days ago?"

"We needed gas and food and motel rooms. Things aren't free, you know," I say.

"You took that out? You knew how to do that?"

"Yeah, you should see. You just put in a number and out spurts the money. It's a great system. I'll show you how to do it when I get home."

"Mom, where are you, exactly? I'm coming out there."

"No, no, Dear. We haven't finished our trip yet. I'll let you know when I'm ready to come home."

There is a pause.

"Have you talked to Carol yet?" he asks.

"Not yet, I'm going to call her next. I love you, Tom."

"I love you too. That's why I need to know where you are."

"Okay. Good-bye." I hang up the phone and start to weep. Rayne puts his arms around me.

"That went pretty well, don't you think?" he says. "What's wrong?"

I try to pull myself together but can't stop the tears. Audrey hands me a Kleenex box and rubs my back. I stare at the phone.

"I need to call Carol. Could you please dial?"

Rayne punches in all the numbers and hands the receiver to me.

"Hello?"

"Hello, Dear."

"Mom? Oh, my God. Mom?"

"Yes. How are you, Carol?"

"I was starting to think I'd never hear your voice again. Where are you?"

"Alberta."

"Mother, really. This isn't a joke. I've been worried sick. Now where are you?"

"I'm in Alberta with Audrey and our friend, Rayne." I pause a moment and listen to sniffles and choking sounds. Carol doesn't reply, so I continue. "We drove here. It's been thrilling. You would have enjoyed it. I'm safe and happy. We have a dog."

Carol regains her composure. "Who are you with?"

"Audrey—you remember Audrey from The Home—and Rayne."

"Rayne? Who's that?"

I struggle to recall how I'd come to know Rayne. He's simply always been here. "He drives the van and knows the way. He talks to us and fills the van with gas and buys food and big yellow flowers, and he saved the dog. He's very kind. You should talk to him."

I hand the receiver to Rayne. He looks terrified.

He puts it to his ear and listens, then begins answering. "Ottawa—in front of the bank—no, it was just a coincidence. I wasn't even thinking about the bank being there—Squamish." He raises his eyebrows and grins slightly as if to reassure me.

"We've talked to the nursing home and your brother already. Everyone knows where we—I don't know, I'm sorry."

His expression becomes much more serious. "I'm only doing what feels right. I didn't know at first that they were running away, or that they had Alzheimer's. We've been together since we left Ottawa—of course we get separate rooms, but other than that, they're always with me."

I can hear Carol's voice, though not the words, becoming shrill and loud. Rayne listens patiently until he can squeeze back into the conversation. "I'm sorry you feel that way. I only did what felt like the best for your mom and Audrey. We're almost to B.C. so I was hoping we could arrange with you to fly them back from Vancouver to Ottawa—"

The voice comes through clearly enough for everyone to hear as I reach for the phone. "No bloody way. You stay right where you are!"

I put the phone to my ear. "Carol, I just wanted to let you know I'm okay."

"Of course," Carol says. "I wish you'd called sooner. It's been a living hell not knowing what happened to you. Did you think about that? The police called but couldn't tell us more than that you were alive. I'm a wreck. I haven't slept or worked since the nursing home called to say you were missing."

I apologize.

"Where are you?" Carol asks. "Where *exactly* are you? I'm coming to get you, and when we get back, I'm moving you here to Toronto so I can keep a closer eye on you. Some place more secure so this doesn't happen again…for your own safety. I didn't realize how determined you could be."

My words come out much more calmly than I could have hoped. "I love you, Carol. I'll call you when we get to Vancouver to let you know what we decide to do."

"Mom, please be reasonable. I love you. We can talk about where you'll live when you get back. How can I get in touch with you?"

"I'll call you. Bye, Dear."

I hang up.

"That was tough," Rayne says. "Are you all right?"

"Mm-hmm." My knees feel like rubber.

I move to the bed. I can't stop the tears. "That...was... awful," I whisper between gulps of air.

"I'm sorry. I guess it wasn't such a good idea," Rayne says. "I thought they'd understand."

"Are we going to call my family?" Audrey asks. "Terry's gone. Maybe my mom or dad?"

Rayne nods. "Your niece, Teresa. They gave me your niece's number. Are you sure you want to do this?"

They move to the phone. The movement of boughs and leaves and shadows outside the window mesmerizes me. I can hear Audrey's voice on the phone, and Rayne's, but only bits and pieces of what they say. Moments later they're back, seated beside me on the bed.

"Teresa was really glad to hear from me," Audrey says. "She's actually Terry's niece—his great-niece, I think. She said she was worried about me."

"She can't come to meet you," Rayne says, "but she's going to call the nursing home and get in touch with Lillian's daughter to see what arrangements they're making. It sounds like she's going to try to have you fly home with Lillian and

Carol and Tom, if they're coming out, and she'll meet you at the airport in Ottawa."

"I wish I had a daughter who would come and meet me."

"I wish I only had a niece who'd just let me be," I say.

"You don't mean that," Audrey says.

"I do."

17

RAYNE LEAVES AND THEN returns with his guitar. He starts quietly, humming along to a few songs that I don't recognize, then, "*Can she bake a cherry pie, Billy Boy, Billy Boy? Can she bake a cherry pie, Charming Billy?*"

Audrey joins in. "*She can bake a cherry pie quick as you can wink your eye, but she's a young thing and cannot leave her mother.*"

Rayne stops playing and smiles.

"Where did you learn that?" Audrey asks.

"My Gran. I can't believe I remember it. It's been a long time. Gran used to sing lots of songs while she cooked and I spent a lot of time eating at her place. I heard them all and I guess I learned them, even though I would have died before admitting it then."

"Sing some more," Audrey says.

Rayne plays a few more songs, figuring out the chords

as he goes along, singing the familiar words of the chorus. Audrey knows all the lyrics. Rayne plays a few songs he has written himself and then sets down the guitar.

I slouch in the comfortable chair. Shadow pads over to the door and whimpers.

"I'm gonna take Shadow for a walk and then go back to my room," Rayne says. "I'll see you in the morning."

"Can we keep Shadow with us tonight?" I ask.

"Sure. She wakes up early to go out though. Are you sure you want her?"

"Yes, please. I'll get up with her if she wants out."

Rayne nods. "Ok. I'll bring her back here when we're done and pick up my guitar."

Audrey and I lounge in the chairs, comfortable, content, not talking just to fill the space. We're like sisters who might have lived together in this room for years.

After some time, Audrey says, "He is really good on that fiddle."

"Guitar."

"That's what I said, guitar."

"We should learn to play. I can sing," I say.

"You're a good singer. You even sing harmony sometimes. I've heard you when the people come in for sing-a-longs for the old folks."

I shiver at the thought of sitting in a room filled with old people in wheelchairs and walkers. At the front, someone hammers out *Roll Out the Barrel* on a piano and someone else tries to lead everyone in song.

"I hate that," I say.

"What?"

"The sing-a-longs. Sing along with the dead-but-not-yet-buried."

"What are you talking about?" Audrey asks. "Who's dead?"

"Me, when I'm in that place." I reach over and hold her hand. "I want to move back home. Why don't you come with me? We'll look after each other."

Audrey sits up straighter in her chair. "Where do you live?"

I pick up my backpack from the bed; rummage around until I find my notepad, then leaf through the pages.

"*Peoples Bank—Albert Street,*" I read. "That must be my bank. I probably live near there. We could find it. We found our way here, didn't we?"

"Are we near Albert Street?" Audrey asks.

"Someone would know." I continue to turn pages, reading the entries. "I don't know what these mean: *Mabel's, campfire, sand and water, yellow curtains.*" I choose words randomly from several pages then look over at Audrey. "Has someone been writing in my book?"

Audrey looks surprised. "No. Who would? You've had it in your purse."

I tuck it back into my bag. I move to the window and watch the river flow through the shallow ravine in the trees. The fading light glints off the swirling water, making it look shiny, like crumpled plastic wrap as it winds between the rocks.

"I remember Mabel's," Audrey says. "That was a long time ago. That cute little girl waited on us, remember?"

I don't remember.

Rayne comes back with Shadow. "She's ready to settle in for the night. Are you sure you want her?" he asks.

"Yes. She's a good girl," Audrey says.

Rayne grips the neck of his guitar and lays the leash on the table. "Goodnight," he says as he closes the door.

Shadow prances back and forth between us, restless at first, searching our faces, wagging her tail.

"I think I'll turn in," Audrey says. She flops down into bed and falls asleep before I even turn around.

I open the window a sliver and lie in bed, gazing at the ceiling. I can hear the rustling leaves and the trucks speed by on the highway. Albert and I sit high in the cab of a big transport truck, hauling sunflowers, driving through the night so the flowers will be fresh when they arrive at their destination. Albert guides the rig along the road, stopping for coffee to keep him alert. I entertain him with stories and jokes, and together, we sing old songs.

A siren wails—an ambulance. The haunting sound grows louder, then fades as it carries Albert away. His heart stopped with no warning.

Blondie stirs between the beds. I roll over and stretch my arm down to rub her side. "Good girl, Blondie," I whisper. "Don't worry, I'm awake with you."

I hear the clicking of toenails on the floor and feel a wet nose nudge my arm.

"Lie down, girl. It's all right."

My back aches with such intensity I can't settle down comfortably. It feels like my spine is made of old metal springs that are rusted and compressed into a solid mass. I wish someone would put me on a mechanical stretcher, like they have in horror movies, and crank it tight until the rust disintegrates and the springs in my spine uncoil.

My head is pounding too, just behind the temples. I roll onto my back and circle my fingers hard against them. I can feel the blood pulsing beneath my fingertips on its way to my brain.

Mom suffered from headaches. I remember her lying in her room, the blinds shut tight, with cold cloths pressed against her forehead. We all knew enough to leave her alone when we saw the room in darkness. Even that bastard, Stuart, always found an excuse to be busy somewhere else. I always wanted to help, running a fresh cloth under cold water and wrapping ice cubes inside, trying to keep my brothers quiet. Susan and Sharon didn't seem to bother. They stayed out of the way when Mom was sick. Where are they now? I haven't seen my sisters or brothers for years. I guess they are staying out of my way, just like they did with Mom.

Audrey starts to snore. The rumbling grows louder, rises in pitch to an abrupt snort and then there's silence. I look over to make sure she's still breathing. The snoring starts again with a low wheeze, a gurgle, then a rumble, and finally, the crowning snort and silence.

I talk quietly to Shadow, "You must think we're crazy old fools, eh Girl? I might even agree with you."

I shuffle over to a chair in the dark, swing my arms around to be sure it's empty and ease down into the cushioned seat. Shapes distinguish themselves in the dark. There is a heap of blankets that must be Audrey and a table near the door that holds a Styrofoam dinner container and coffee cup. Another easy chair stands beside mine, and the bathroom door is slightly ajar. I'm oddly at home in this unlit room. My headache subsides, leaving only a dull discomfort behind my eyes and the back pain that accompanies me always.

I was never alone when I was young—no room for such luxury with seven kids and two adults in one small house. I was in the middle, three older and three younger, and I liked my place in the family just fine. I could be invisible if I wanted, lost amid the crowd, but if I wanted attention or needed help, there was always someone there. There weren't a lot of brawls except when Gordon stole Bill's girlfriend, or Wesley told someone that John was afraid of thunder storms; things like that. But later, we must have fallen out of touch. I can't remember getting together with my family after they all married and had children or even if the others married at all. Could that be right? Am I the only one who has an Albert?

I try to picture Albert now but can't. I close my eyes. Nothing. I breathe deeply, trying to catch his scent. I wrap my arms tightly across my chest and hold onto my shoulders, completely alone.

I rest my head back in the chair and stare at the tile ceiling.

A phone is jangling—loud and persistent. My eyes follow the sound to the far side of the room; I struggle to get out of the chair. One of the beds is piled high with blankets. One flowered sleeve pokes out near the top of the mound. The phone continues to ring as I make my way toward it, hobbling between the pieces of furniture that support my weight. I only want to stop the noise from crashing into my head. I pick up the receiver and hold it to my ear.

"Mom? Hello? Lillian Gorsen?"

"Who is this?" I ask.

"Mom, it's Carol. I'm so glad you're still there."

"Of course I'm here," I say, "though God knows where 'here' is." I glance again around the room.

"That's exactly why I'm calling. I had the phone company trace your call, and they said it was from a motel near Medicine Hat. I can't tell you how relieved I am that you're still there."

"It's the middle of the night, Dear. Of course I'm still here."

"Sorry. I forgot the time difference. It's early morning here. Listen, I've booked a flight to Calgary and then a smaller plane to get me to Medicine Hat late tonight. I need you to stay there until I arrive. Do you understand?"

I'm speechless.

"Mom, are you there?"

"Yes."

"Is that man there—Rayne? Could I speak to him?"

I look around again, focusing on the face now clearly resting on a pillow near the flowered arm. "He's not here," I say, "only Audrey is here and she's sleeping. Do you want me to wake her?"

"No. No, just let her sleep. Listen Mom, this is really important. You need to stay where you are until I get there. I have to leave for the airport to catch my flight. I'll call you later. Do you understand?"

"Why do you keep asking me that? You want me to stay here until you get here, right?"

"That's right. I'll be there late tonight, around midnight."

Shadow is now sitting in front of me, whimpering.

"I need to take the dog out," I say.

"That's fine, just don't drive anywhere. Book the room for another night, okay? Stick around there today, and I'll see you soon."

219

"Why?" I form the word slowly and carefully.

"Because I'm coming to get you to bring you home. You need to get back, start taking your meds again, and settle into a place where you're safe."

"You're taking me home to live with you?"

There is a brief silence, then, "Not exactly, we're going to find you a nice nursing home in Toronto so I can be closer to you. We'll talk about it when I see you. It'll be better."

"No. That's not what I want." I don't know what else to say and I don't want to listen to her anymore. I hang up the phone and stare at the metal-framed print on the wall—a snow-capped mountain scene with a lake beyond. It is so ordinary, so unexceptional and yet I can't take my eyes off of it. Shadow nudges my leg and lies down, her chin resting on my foot.

I stand very still, leaning on the desk, my chest constricted, head throbbing. I'm not exactly sure where I am, but it's safe and comfortable. Rumbling snores roll from beneath the blankets on the nearby bed and I know instinctively they belong to a friend. The weight on my foot reminds me of the connection I have with this beautiful pup, who seems always to be with me. My hand touches the phone and bits of conversation slam back. My daughter wants me to go to a nursing home in a strange city. It makes my legs wobbly and my palms sweaty. Where would Audrey be if I lived in Toronto? How would I get to work and how would my friends find me? And what about Albert—his job—no, he's buried in Ottawa. I need to be near him. It simply won't work.

A band of light plays across Shadow's back. The first signs of dawn sliver in between the curtains.

Shadow rises and clicks toward the door, tail wagging in anticipation.

The pair of pants I wore yesterday is now draped over the foot of the bed. I pull them on underneath my yellow nightgown. I tug at the corner of a purple sweater buried deep in my pack and wriggle into it. The sleeves of my nightgown scrunch up inside, bulging like huge muscles so that I can hardly bend my arms, and I give up trying after securing the two middle buttons. I sit down to lace up my shoes.

"Whew, that was a lot of work," I say to Shadow. "Now, where's your leash?"

Outside, the sun is just visible on the horizon, turning the sky to denim, promising a beautiful day. Shadow squats immediately, then darts from side-to-side, straining at the end of her leash and pulling me along.

"Hold on, Girl. Slow down," I say, gripping tightly with both hands.

Shadow eases back but doesn't stop, sniffs the ground and air, leads me toward the trees and onto a path. The scent of pine and night-damp wood envelopes me and, I am in Algonquin Park.

Albert brushes past. He ducks inside a tent and opens the flap, calls to me, "Come see the surprise I have for you, sexy lady." He flashes his buck-naked body at me, all pink and erect, ready.

I move toward him and stumble. The ground is uneven. I choose each footstep carefully, edging down the slope with the help of branches, stumps, and tree trunks, holding tightly onto the leash with my other hand. The muffled sounds of traffic hum in the distance.

"Albert?" I call. Where has he gone? "Albert, don't let anyone else see you like that."

At the bottom of the woodlot, a river swirls by, tumbling
over rocks that lie visible just below the surface, crashing
headlong into other, bigger boulders and a fallen tree. The
water moves swiftly, eddying around the branches that still
cling to the trunk of the tree whose roots must have recently
pulled away from the bank and sent it crashing into the water.

I stand on a cushion of crunchy pine needles and brown
matted leaves, a little way from the water's edge. I am surprised at the river's force.

Shadow tugs gently, stretching forward to drink. I teeter
back and forth, dizzied by the swift movement of the water.
I take a step closer and lean against the exposed roots of the
fallen tree. A heaviness settles back over me. It feels all wrong.
I am my own person now with new friends, making my own
choices, and it's good. I'm on an adventure, and Carol's call, her
coming here to get me, is going to bring it all crashing down.

But she is family. I should always make time for my
daughter. Carol isn't here now though—or is she? Yes, she's
on her way. I could hide. There are plenty of places here that
I could tuck into, and no one would find me.

We're going to find you a nice nursing home in Toronto.
I don't want to go back there—nurses wearing surgical gloves,
scrubbing my armpits and privates with a scratchy washcloth,
rinsing me off with a hose, a bed with railings, and Jell-O and
pudding and green beans every day, and I don't want to go
somewhere new.

The sky is getting brighter. The air is still. The water is
clear despite its churning motion, the riverbank along the

edge a scree of stones and rocks, gray and brown with flecks of deep red and gold. It looks like the bottom drops off near the middle, partially hidden by swirls and reflections.

Shadow stands taut and ready to dive after anything that catches her interest, eyes riveted just below the surface of the water.

Bending over, I run my hand along Shadow's spine, drawing the dog's attention back. I smile at the intensity in her face. "You're a good girl," I say. Shadow's tensed muscles relax and she moves to my side. I stroke her back again and again, soaking up the warmth in my hand and stopping to feel the heartbeat, steady and strong beneath her ribs.

I straighten up and look again at the river, my mind buzzing and addled, then suddenly calm and clear.

I wrap the end of the leash around one of the roots. I lean over again and unlace my shoes, take them off, and set them side-by-side on the tree trunk, bright blue and yellow against the browns. I pull off my socks and tuck them inside the shoes, then stand and steady myself.

"Shadow, you stay," I say, unclipping the leash from the collar. She remains seated. "Stay girl," I repeat.

I walk several steps upriver to a place where the bank slopes more gradually into the water. I glance back at Shadow and hold up my hand in a stay gesture, then turn and step into the water.

At first the cold sends a piercing warning up my legs, and I have to maneuver to keep my balance on the loose stones. I stand for a moment in the frigid waters of Algonquin Park.

Part III

Flown

18

ALBERT CALLS OUT to me again. "Lillian, where are you?"

I twist around to see him. He isn't there but Shadow is. I can see the window of the motel room where Audrey is resting. She trusts me. She's so confused sometimes. I need to get out of this water and stop acting like a child; a defeated, compulsive child.

My feet start to cramp. I teeter on the slippery stones, unable to turn around, terrified of falling forward into the deeper part of the river. The current pulls at my thighs. From the corner of my eye, I see Shadow run toward me and leap into the water. Before she reaches me, she is carried downstream.

I hear a scream. I think it might be mine. I step backward toward the riverbank but lose my footing and topple. My heart crashes through my chest as the cold water surges around me, yellow fabric billowing around my chin, a purple woolly weight tugging my arms under.

My hip drags and bumps along the bottom. My head, like a buoy, floats above the surface, safe except for a few splashes and sloshes that fill my mouth and sting my eyes. The fallen tree stretches out in front of me. I swirl with the current, bobbing and spinning like a bathtub boat and crash to an abrupt stop, wedged in the crook of a big branch.

I hold on with all my strength. Breathe. The riverbank looks so close, twigs and dead leaves from the fallen tree are scattered there. Everything is bigger, stronger, clearer than it should be. I can smell the decay, the clay, the moss.

My fingers are curled around the branch, arms frozen here, clenched inside the sleeves of my sweater. The river pummels me farther and farther into the tree. I can see through the canopy of leaves above that the sky is now brightening toward dawn.

Rayne runs toward me. He doesn't even slow down at the water's edge, just wades in, untangles me from the tree's hold, and pulls me to the shore. I'm amazed at his strength. He's such a scrawny fellow, especially standing over me, soaked to the hide, vacuum-packed inside soaking wet clothes and hair.

"Jesus, Lillian! What the hell were you doing?"

I try to raise my head but it's turned into a leaden cannon ball. I need to sleep. It's all I can think about.

I'm in bed with blankets heaped on top of me. I can hear Rayne and Audrey. I know they're there, but I can't wake up. Rayne sounds frantic. He keeps shaking me, trying to make me open my eyes. I hate him for this. All I want to do is sleep.

I'm sitting on the edge of the bathtub and Audrey is helping me get undressed. She isn't talking, just stripping off layers of wet clothes. I drag my legs up over the side; ease myself down into the warm water.

She touches my face gently with the back of her fingers. "You look like you were in a fight. You're black-and-blue."

"And red all over," I say. She sits there forever while I soak, and my blood starts to circulate again. "Help me out of here, please. The water is starting to get cold."

In the other room, Rayne is very quiet. Shadow lies on the floor, not making a sound. I've let everyone down. I can tell. I don't know what I was thinking, but it won't happen again. We need to keep going.

"What are we waiting for?" I say. "Why is everyone so glum? Come on. Let's pack up and get moving. We have things to see."

Rayne piles everything into the van and helps me into my seat. This time I let him. Lightning bolts shoot through my hips and my arms hang like day-old balloons—the long sausage kind, deflated and dimpled in shades of pink and purple.

Rayne's eyes are heavy. His shoulders slope downward. There is something hovering over him that I didn't notice before: disappointment or maybe fear.

"I'm fine, Dear. Don't worry about me," I say. "I slipped. That's all. I'm a little shaky on my feet sometimes."

Along the highway, the air is hot and still in the van.

"Can you open the window, please?" I ask. With that, a warm wind swirls around me, catching my hair and whipping it back. I feel like a kid on a bike, legs stretched up and out to the sides, happy, wanting nothing more than this.

I want Audrey to feel it too. "Audrey, open your window

and reach your hand out," I shout to be heard above the roar of wind in my ears.

"I don't want to," she says.

"Don't be like that. It feels great."

She doesn't look back. "I should have been there. Was it Terry that hurt you?"

"No. No, I slipped and fell. No one touched me."

Audrey starts to cry. "I'm worried and scared. We're too far from home. I don't even know where we are."

"We're on the road, Honey. That's where we are. We're going somewhere," I say.

Rayne reaches over and touches Audrey's hand. "By mid-afternoon, we'll be passing by Calgary. Keep watching and you'll see the city skyline. I want you to look just beyond that."

He looks at me in the rearview mirror. "You okay?"

"Mm-hmm." My hips are screaming. I try to ignore them. "I'd like some butterscotch ice cream, please."

"We'll find some later," Rayne says.

Hours and hours pass. I can't tell if I'm sleeping or awake. My eyes feel scratchy and blurry in turns and then, don't feel like anything at all. My heart thumps loudly through my eardrums and sweat pools in the center of my back. My cheeks burn as if I'd spent too much time in the sun. A cramp grips my belly, pulls me suddenly forward, leaves my head resting in my hands. A moan escapes from way down in my gut without warning.

Rayne pulls over to the shoulder of the road and jumps out. The side door slides open and he touches my shoulder, rubs in tentative little circles and bends over to see my face.

"What's wrong?" he asks. "You're starting to scare me. Do we need to get you to a hospital?"

Audrey struggles with her seatbelt, cursing the whole time. She frees herself and twists around to look at me. "You're beet-red!"

I'm feverish and dizzy. Rayne pushes Shadow into the back and helps me swing my feet up onto the seat. He tucks something under my head and I curl up on my side. The van swirls around me. My eyes refuse to stay open.

Someone is calling my name. A uniform stands at the door of the van with a wheelchair. One hand cradles my head and the other, my shoulder.

"Can you sit up, Ma'am?"

I try to push myself up, but my body is too heavy. My arm buckles under me. Heat swirls in from outside, the smell of hot pavement mixes with air conditioning.

Rayne's voice is rising and falling with *unconscious* and *fever* and *slipped and fell*, Audrey's with *vacation* and *far from home*.

"We live together," I hear her say, "in Ottawa."

Someone helps me into a wheelchair. My hips—no, just my right hip—hurts like hell. I'm wheeled into the Emergency Room, right past the desk, past people with grouchy looks on their faces, who turn their attention from the television screen long enough to gawk at me. Audrey follows us through.

"Please have a seat in the waiting room," the uniform says to Audrey and Rayne.

"But she may need help remembering," Rayne says. "She has Alzheimer's."

231

The uniform points back toward the entrance. "We'll come and get you if we need you. Please have a seat in the waiting room."

Audrey follows us in and plops down in the chair beside my gurney.

"Ma'am," the uniform says, "please wait outside with your friend."

"No thank you," Audrey says. "I'll wait here."

The uniform clenches her jaw. I don't think she's used to being contradicted, but she seems to know better than to argue with Audrey.

"Do you have a health card, Mrs. Gorsen?"

I don't know what she means. Birthday card? Anniversary card? It doesn't make sense. "No, Dear. I have no cards."

"No health card? Your friend said you live in Ottawa. Is that right?"

"I don't know." I turn to Audrey, but she is absorbed in reading the labels on all the packages on a shelf near her chair. She ignores the question about cards. She probably doesn't have any either.

"Can you tell me why you're here?" the woman asks.

Again, I'm not quite sure what she means. Here in the hospital or in whatever city we're in? I try to explain. "We're in the van because the car isn't ours. It's more comfortable anyway. I fell. I know that. My hip is throbbing like a giant toothache. It's making me feel like I'm sitting on an angle and I'm going to topple over. Can you do anything about that?"

"I need to get you registered before we can do anything else. The young man said your name is Lillian Gorsen. Is that right?"

I just look at her. I'm not sure anymore.

"I'll need some identification. Can you have a look through your pack there please?"

She unzips the backpack and sets it on my lap. I pull back as the scent of dirty laundry, urine, and sweat, hits me. These can't be my clothes. They smell like some of the men at the nursing home who wear the same outfit every day. Not me. I hand the pack back to the uniform.

"Is this not yours?" she asks.

Audrey answers. "Yes. Remember Lillian? It's yours."

The nurse nods. "Maybe we'd better ask the young man to come in here and clear this up."

I'm starting to feel nauseous. "Can't we just move this along? I need someone to look at my hip before I pass out with the pain. Why is it taking so long?"

She shifts the head of the bed down a bit and stuffs pillows behind my lower back and under my knees. I lean back to test this new position. Better, but my hip still hurts.

"Lillian," the uniform says, "this fall you had, did anyone push you or cause you to slip?"

"No." I try to remember the details. There was water. I remember that. I was cold and wet. "I was swimming. My sisters and I were swimming and diving off the raft that Dad built. No. It was Albert. Albert built the raft."

The uniform turns to Audrey, but she just shakes her head. "I don't know. I worried that Terry might have pushed her, but she said no."

"Terry? Who's Terry?" the uniform asks.

"My husband. He's dead now."

The woman pats Audrey on the shoulder and leaves the

room. I'm so glad that Audrey's here. We understand each other. I just need to know she's in the room; that she's near if anything should happen. I feel responsible too, responsible for Audrey's safety. We're friends and we need to stick together.

Something is hissing and beeping, bumping and rolling behind the curtain. A cloud of sleep floats just beyond my head. I try to open my eyes, but my eyelids are heavy, locked tight. I fight harder to wake up. I need to be sure my friend hasn't gone somewhere while I've slept.

There she is. I breathe deeply, filling my lungs with oxygen. I relax a bit. Audrey is curled up under a blanket in a bed right beside mine. Someone must have rolled another cot into the draped rectangle that is now my room. But there is something missing. I try to focus. Something. I feel around the bed for my green and purple quilt. It's gone. I can't think when I've last seen it.

The fluorescent lights are out and I can feel that afternoon has turned into evening. There's a small commotion outside the curtains, a voice I should recognize but can't quite place.

"Where is she? Can I see her?"

The uniform leads a woman into our enclosure, and I'm surprised to see that it's Carol. She is standing beside me. Tears are rolling down her cheeks, and she's wiping them away just as fast as they appear.

"Mom. I'm so glad you're all right. The nurse told me what happened. I can't believe you held on; that you survived in that river."

I don't know what she's talking about. I try to sit up but can't. She rubs my arm and gives me a hug.

"Just rest. You're going to be fine. Your hip is just badly bruised."

Audrey rustles about. She rolls onto her back and smiles. "I see we have company," she says. "Hello. I'm Audrey."

"Hello, Audrey. Nice to see you again. Carol."

"Carol? Our daughter?" Audrey says. She looks around the room, her forehead scrunched into a frown. "Are we home?"

"No, not yet," Carol says. "Soon. I took an early morning flight to Calgary and your friend, Rayne, caught up with me by phone before I got on the plane to Medicine Hat to tell me that you and Mom were here in the hospital. I got here as quickly as I could."

Audrey smiled. "I love that boy. Where is he?"

The uniformed woman answers. "He left a while ago. He told us the story of what had happened, and then he contacted Lillian's daughter and son and your niece. After he spoke to them and he knew you'd be okay, he said he had to leave. He asked me to give you this envelope."

Inside, there is a small bundle of twenties and a note. *"Sorry. This is from Blazing Sevens. I'm not sure why I held onto it. Didn't spend any, but kept enough for gas to get home. Rayne."*

"Where did he go?" Audrey asks.

"I'm not sure. He just said he had to go," the uniform says. She turns to Carol. "I'll leave you to help them get dressed. Take as long as you need."

Carol is looking at me now, and I am watching her, plotting our next move.

"Carol, Dear, I'm glad you're here. We could use a new driver since Albert has jumped ship and taken Blondie with him. It will be scrumptious having you along. We don't do enough together, mother and daughter—and Audrey, of course. Wouldn't you agree?"

"Mom, you know that's not possible, don't you?"

"I know nothing of the sort."

Carol helps me sit up, kneels and fits shoes onto my feet, laces them tight. "Where's your sweater? You'll need it. The evenings are cooler out here." She turns to Audrey and helps her with shoes as well. "Come on, you two. I'm taking you home. There's a red-eye flight heading east with a few empty seats, and we're going to be on it."

Audrey's eyes light up. "A plane? I've never been on a plane. Come on, Lillian. This is gonna be great."

My hip whines and complains as I ease down from the gurney onto wobbly legs. Carol takes my hand and gently draws it through the crook of her elbow, supporting me, keeping me close.

The nurse insists I ride in the wheelchair, and I think that maybe, just this once, I'll go along. And so we leave here, bags piled on my lap, nurse wheeling me to the door, Audrey holding her cane with one hand, Carol's arm with the other.

We're in a rental car on the way to the airport. Carol is driving. Audrey is still moping about Rayne being gone. I say good riddance. The boy has issues. We could have done it without him.

"Will the plane fly over the mountains on the way to B.C.?" Audrey asks.

"We're not going to B.C. Audrey. We're going back to Ontario," Carol says in a voice that sounds too soft to be Carol's.

"And we'll need to have a long talk about where you will be living," she says to me.

"Talk all you want, Dear. I'm not going to another *Home*."

"We'll see," she says, glancing at me quickly and then returning her attention to the road.

"You bet we will," I say. "We'll see, indeed." I pat the envelope that bulges in my pocket, search through my pack for my pen and pad. I need to make a note. So I don't forget.

ACKNOWLEDGMENTS

I gratefully acknowledge the support of Ontario Arts Council for its financial assistance during the completion of this book.

I would also like to extend many thanks to Erika de Vasconcelos and Harold Rhenisch, for help with parts of this manuscript at its various stages, and to Carolyn Jackson and Margie Wolfe at Second Story Press and Kathryn Cole, for their thoughtful editorial suggestions, their wisdom and encouragement. I wish to acknowledge the help of Allan Briesmaster, who gave insight and guidance regarding the details of a good query letter and the value of persistence. I am grateful to first readers Gary, Jordi, Jon, and Gavin, Barb Hourigan, Liz Barrett-Milner, Kit Julian, Jane Goodlet, Jane and Dave Beckett, Jody Overend, and Amber Homeniuk. I am most thankful to Gary for his extraordinary support, unwavering optimism and good humor, and to our children, Jordi and Jon, for their constant and spirited inspiration.

I would like to acknowledge the use of lyrics for "Side by Side," Gus Kahn, 1927, and for "You Are My Sunshine," copyright 1940, Peer International Corporation, by Jimmy Davis and Charles Mitchell.

ABOUT THE AUTHOR

Janet Hepburn is a writer and poet whose work has appeared in numerous publications. She was shortlisted in the FreeFall 2011 Annual Poetry and Prose Contest and has been a regular contributor to a regional weekly newspaper, writing personal life stories of passion and success. Her travel stories have been published online. *Flee, Fly, Flown* is her first novel. She lives and works in Port Dover, Ontario.